MY WONDERFUL TREASURY OF
115 FIVE-MINUTE
BEDTIME STORIES

This edition is published by Armadillo, an imprint of Anness Publishing Ltd,
108 Great Russell Street, London WC1B 3NA; info@anness.com

www.annesspublishing.com

If you like the images in this book and would like to investigate using them for publishing, promotions or advertising,
please visit our website www.practicalpictures.com for more information.

© Anness Publishing Ltd 2014

A CIP catalogue record for this book is available from the British Library.

Publisher: Joanna Lorenz
Editor: Elizabeth Young
Production Controller: Mai-Ling Collyer

Previously published as *My Treasury of Five Minute Stories*

PUBLISHER'S NOTE
The author and publishers have made every effort to ensure that this book is safe for its intended use, and cannot
accept any legal responsibility or liability for any harm or injury arising from misuse.

Manufacturer: Anness Publishing Ltd, 108 Great Russell Street, London WC1B 3NA, England
For Product Tracking go to: www.annesspublishing.com/tracking
Batch: 6073-23023-1127

MY WONDERFUL TREASURY OF
115 FIVE-MINUTE
BEDTIME STORIES

WRITTEN BY NICOLA BAXTER • ILLUSTRATED BY JENNY PRESS

ARMADILLO

Introduction

Children and grown-ups alike will love this charming collection of short stories. Separated into four chapters, there is something for everyone, with bouncing bears, funny farmyard animals, cuddly kittens and lots more amazing characters to meet:

Five-Minute Teddy Bear Tales
The little town of Bearborough is home to as fine a bunch of bears as you could ever hope to meet. There are baby bears and granny bears, opera-singing bears, and trampolining bears!

Five-Minute Farmyard Tales
There's always something happening down on Windytop Farm. There are lambs that sing, ducks that cluck, and even pigs that fly! And there are dozens of animals all wondering how Farmer Barnes is ever going to find a wife.

Five-Minute Kitten Tales
When a mother has five little kittens to take care of, she certainly has her paws full! She just can't keep her eyes on them all at once.

Five-Minute Bedtime Tales
There is something for everyone in this enchanting collection of sleepytime stories. There are sensible mice, silly rabbits, noisy elves, and blue elephants . . . and lots of surprises.

Contents

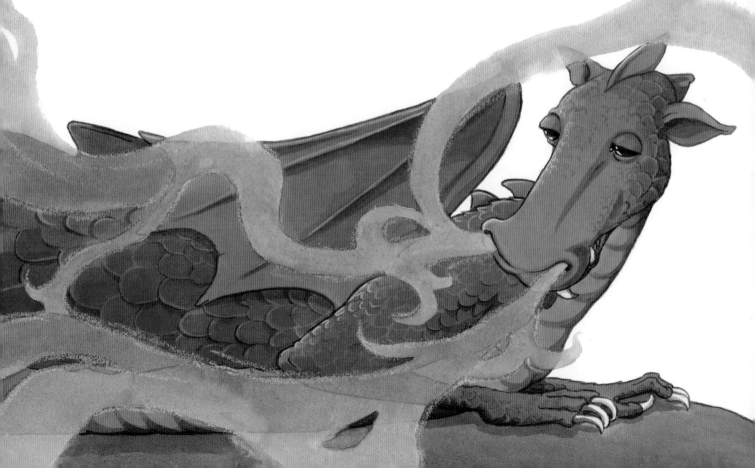

Five-Minute Teddy Bear Tales

Meet the Teddy Bears!

Here are some of the very fine bears you will meet in
the little town of Bearborough.

Percival

Mrs Bear   Granny

Bertram   Mr Bear

Max   Cleo

Barney

Contents

Bedtime for Little Bears

All little bears love to snuggle down in their beds at night and go to sleep. When their little heads are on their pillows, they dream of honey and cake and teddy bear games. But before they go to bed, little bears must have their baths, and *some* little bears just do not like to get their ears wet!

Once there was a little bear called Barney, who really *hated* his bath. His father tried everything to make bathtime fun. He bought a huge boat for Barney to play with. But Barney complained that there was no room in the tub for *him*! So Barney's father bought a bottle of the biggest bubbles you have ever seen. In fact, it was fairly difficult to see that little bear at all. The bubbles floated and sparkled and burst with a *pop!* But Barney said that they tickled his nose, so they had to go.

Three yellow ducks, a water wheel, and some stuff that turned the water purple didn't work either.

One day, Barney went for a walk with his granny. As they walked, it started to rain. Luckily, Barney was wearing his boots and Granny was carrying her umbrella. But right away, Barney started to complain.

"I don't like getting wet," he whined. "It gets in my ears and in my eyes and up my nose, and it's *horrible*."

"Well, Barney, I am surprised," said Granny, "that you would want to give up all that good luck."

"Good luck?" asked Barney. "What do you mean?"

"I thought all little bears knew about it," Granny replied. "Didn't you know that every drop of water that touches you is a little bit of good luck that will follow you all your life? I always try to get as wet as possible." And Granny threw away her umbrella and started to splash in the puddles!

The next night at bathtime, Barney's father was surprised to find that Barney jumped right into the tub with no fuss at all. In fact, it was difficult to make him get out and snuggle down in his little bed. And I have heard that nowadays Barney is the luckiest little bear you have ever met – and the cleanest!

Big Bears, Little Bears

One afternoon, Barney and his friend Cleo were playing in the park, when some bigger bears came along.

"We want to play on the swings, baby bears," they said rudely. "Get lost!"

Barney was not a very brave little bear, but he didn't want to look silly in front of Cleo, so he spoke up loudly.

"We were here first," he said, "but we could go on the merry-go-round instead, if you like. We've been on the swings for a long time now."

But as soon as Barney and Cleo were whizzing around on the merry-go-round, the bigger bears came along and wanted to play on that too. They weren't nice about it.

Cleo didn't want any trouble. "Let's go and play with our kite, Barney," she said. "They can have the swings and the merry-go-round and everything to themselves."

Barney agreed at once.

Soon the little bears were playing happily. It was a windy day that was perfect for kite-flying. But before long, the big bears began to run around playing ball. The park was plenty big enough for everyone, but they insisted on running close to the little bears. Barney was afraid that one of them would get tangled up in the kite string, or worse still, bump into him so that he let go and his kite went flying off by itself.

Just then, there was a huge gust of wind, and things happened at once. The big bears' ball blew under the merry-go-round and the little bears' kite flew into a tree. Now neither the little bears nor the big bears could play.

Barney was ready to start for home, but Cleo, who was a very clever little bear, had an idea.

"You big bears are tall enough to reach our kite," she said. "And we are small enough to crawl under the merry-go-round and get your ball. What do you think?"

The big bears shuffled their feet and looked ashamed.

"We're sorry we teased you," they said. "It's a very good idea."

So the little bears crawled, and the big bears stretched, and everyone played happily together for the rest of the afternoon.

The Blue Bear

In a neat little house in the middle of Bearborough there lived a very silly bear. The problem with Albert was that he always had to have the very latest things. He was so eager to keep up with fashion that when he saw his friends and relatives he would say, "Oh dear, my cousin Jackson is wearing last month's jacket. Only three buttons instead of six on his coat, too. Poor Jackson. Poor bear!"

To be fair, Albert's clothes were sometimes extraordinarily wonderful, but more often he simply looked extraordinarily silly.

Each month, Albert's fashion magazines arrived in the mail. Usually they confirmed that he was the best dressed bear in town. On this particular morning, Albert couldn't wait to tear open the enormous package of magazines that had just arrived.

But when he glanced at the covers, he gave a groan of despair. *Blue!* Everything must be blue! It seemed that nothing else would do at all.

Albert looked at his wardrobe with tears in his eyes. There were orange clothes and purple clothes. There were green and yellow striped hats and pink and black spotted socks. All of them would have to go! What a waste!

But that evening in bed, Albert had an inspiration. What if he could dye all his clothes? Then he would be the height of fashion without spending too much money. It was brilliant!

Albert had so many clothes, he decided that only the ornamental pool in his garden would be big enough to dye them in. Luckily, there were no fish in it. Albert tipped in pack after pack of dye. The water became bright blue. Then he hurried to his bedroom to begin carrying out the clothes.

It was unfortunate that he tried to carry so many at once. It was even more unfortunate that he had left a watering can on the path. Before he could stop himself, Albert was sailing through the air to land with a *splash!* in the pond.

You can guess what happened. Albert was dyed blue from ears to paws. At last, thought his friends, trying not to laugh, he will have learned his lesson about keeping up with fashion.

But Albert's friends were wrong. Albert loved his new blue fur – for a while. I hear now that fashion has changed, and stripes are all the rage. Let me put it this way . . . you won't find it hard to spot Albert next time you come to Bearborough!

The Bear on the Bus

Wednesday was market day in Bearborough. From all the surrounding farms and villages, bears flooded into town. Of course, bears came to town in all sorts of ways. They wobbled on bicycles and tricycles. They rattled along in vans and trucks. But lots of bears hopped onto the bus, which was always full to bursting.

One Wednesday morning, Barney and his granny caught the bus into town. They had a lovely time. When it was time to come home, they once again waited for the bus and squeezed onto it with lots of other bears.

"It's standing room only, I'm afraid," said Granny, "but I'll hold you up if you like, Barney, so you can see out of the window."

But Barney soon found that the bear standing in front of him was much more interesting than what was outside the windows. He was an elderly bear, wearing a hat. That was

not very strange, for lots of older bears wear hats. What *was* very odd was that Barney was sure he had seen the hat move!

Barney looked hard at the back of the bear's head. There it was again! The hat gave a little jiggle, as though it was dancing.

Barney was fascinated. The hat jiggled again. The little bear wriggled in Granny's arms with excitement.

"Keep still, Barney," said Granny. "I'll drop you if you're not careful."

"But Granny," whispered Barney, "look!" And he pointed at the bear's hat.

Just then, the hat seemed to bounce on the bear's head. Granny was so surprised that she gave a little scream, and the bear in front turned around.

"My dear lady," he cried, "can I help you in any way?"

Wordlessly, Granny pointed to his hat. The bear smiled. "I should introduce myself," he said. "I am Bertram Bear, and this," he went on, gallantly doffing his hat, "is my friend Percival."

Granny and Barney laughed aloud when they saw the little mouse sitting on the old bear's head.

"I hope that we will all be the best of friends," said Bertram, smiling at Granny.

Teddy Bear Time

When a visitor to Bearborough last year asked some local bears for the time, as her watch had stopped – she got some strange answers.

"Half past three," the bear who sells fruit and vegetables said, glancing up at the Town Hall clock.

"A quarter to nine," the bear in the bakery replied, looking at the clock high on the church.

"Nine minutes after five," the bear who sells ice cream on the corner of the main street said, peering at the clock on top of the train station.

You have probably guessed that all the clocks in Bearborough were wrong. That was because old Mr Minim, the only clock mender in town, had become a little shaky on his legs. Although fit and well in every other way, he simply could not face climbing up a ladder to mend clocks high up.

As you can imagine, the clocks really were a problem. The trains were never on time, and the shopkeepers didn't know when to open their shops.

Then, one day, Bearborough had two very special visitors. They were a bear called Alfred and his friend Jumble – who was an elephant! Now most bears in Bearborough had never seen an elephant before, so they all gathered round. And the elephant, pleased to show off his size and strength, wrapped his trunk around each of the little bears in turn and lifted them up high, squealing with excitement.

"Excuse me, Jumble," said Mr Minim, tapping him lightly on the toe with his walking stick. "Could you lift a grown-up bear, like me, for example?"

In seconds, Mr Minim found himself dangling above the crowd, yet he felt as safe as if he was standing on firm ground.

And that is why, if you visit Bearborough these days, all the clocks are exactly right, for Jumble visits every twelve months, and Mr Minim always says that's the *high*light of his year!

Uncle Hugo's Invention

Cleo's Uncle Hugo lived in a ramshackle old house on the edge of Bearborough. When Cleo first took him to visit, Barney was rather afraid of the old bear. He wasn't used to bears who talked in gruff voices and didn't seem to know what day of the week it was.

But Barney soon found that Uncle Hugo's house was one of the most exciting he had ever been in. There was a stuffed alligator in the hall and a real live parrot in the living room. There were collections of fossils and piles of books everywhere. For Uncle Hugo was the kind of bear who gets very enthusiastic about something – before he forgets all about it.

Uncle Hugo was passionate about his new invention. It was the most extraordinary-looking machine.

"Er . . . excuse me, sir," stammered Barney. "What exactly does it do?"

"It whistles," said Uncle Hugo briefly.

"Whistles?" Cleo was just as puzzled.

"Yes," said her uncle. "I got the idea when the kettle boiled one day. It made a lovely whistling noise, so I thought I could make a machine that would whistle in tune."

Neither Barney nor Cleo were very good at whistling. The machine sounded wonderful.

"Now," cried Uncle Hugo, "for the moment of truth. I turn this switch here, and open this valve here, and the water in the boiler will start to bubble and steam. Then prepare yourselves for a wonderful sound."

Sure enough, there soon came a bubbling, followed by a whooshing, and then, yes, there was a sound that would make any young bear grin with delight. But it wasn't the sound of whistling. Oh no. It was the sound of Uncle Hugo zooming across the room on his machine and crashing straight through the doors that led into the garden.

When Barney and Cleo rushed outside, they found Uncle Hugo and his machine sitting in the middle of a rose bed.

"Hmm," said the old bear. "It's not, in fact, a whistling machine after all. It's a steam-driven mowing machine, and it works perfectly! Just look at my lawn!"

And Uncle Hugo was so happy that he began to . . . whistle.

The Snow Bear

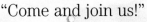

W hen heavy snow fell on the town of
Bearborough, Cleo's little brother
really wanted to go out and play in it.
But he still had a bad cold, so Cleo's
mother said he must stay indoors.

"Don't worry, Max," said Cleo
kindly. "I'll build you a beautiful snow
bear right in front of the window where
you can see it all day."

No sooner had Cleo started piling up the snow, when
Barney came past, pulling his sled.

"Can I play too?" he asked. "I bet I could build a better
snow bear than you!"

"Just you come and try!" retorted Cleo.

Well, before long, several other little bears came along.

"What are you doing?" they called.

"We're having a snow bear competition," cried Barney.
"Come and join us!"

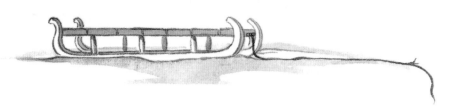

Soon, much to Max's delight, there were five little bears building snow bears in Cleo's garden.

Everyone was very busy – except Barney. He soon decided to take a rest by throwing snowballs into the branches of the trees. It was fun when the snow lying high up came down with a *whoosh!* The other little bears were too busy making their snow bears to notice.

After about an hour, the bears had finished. Five fine snow bears stood in a row in the garden. Cleo's mother agreed to be the judge of the competition, and Max pointed excitedly to help her make the right choice.

"There's no doubt about it," she said after a careful look at the snow bears. "The one at the end is certainly the best."

"It must be Barney's bear," said Cleo, "but where is he?"

Just then, there was a muffled giggle, and Barney's bear collapsed in a heap – with Barney inside it!

"The snow from that tree fell right on top of me," he laughed. "Didn't I make a good snow bear?"

"I can't award a prize for an accident!" laughed Cleo's mother. "You can all have a prize of hot cocoa. Come inside now!"

Follow the Rainbow

On Saturday mornings, lots of little bears went to the library for Story Time. Mr Leaf, the librarian, asked them all to sit down in a circle, while he read to them from one of the beautiful books on the shelves.

One morning, Mr Leaf read a story in which a pixie found a pot of gold at the end of a rainbow. Barney was very interested, especially when he noticed that it was raining outside.

When the children were ready to go home, the rain had stopped, although there were lots of lovely puddles for them to splash in.

But Barney didn't want to stop and splash. "Come on!" he said to Cleo, pulling her along. "We've got to hurry!" And he dragged the poor little bear along Main Street.

As soon as the tallest buildings were left behind, the two bears could see that there was a beautiful rainbow in the sky.

"Quick!" cried Barney. "We've got to find the end before it disappears!"

"But Barney! . . ." Cleo's sensible words were lost as her friend rushed along.

"Look!" cried Barney a few moments later. He could hardly believe his eyes. There was no doubt about it. As they reached the top of the hill that led down to Barney's house, they could clearly see the end of the rainbow. And it was right in the middle of his front garden!

Barney and Cleo flew down the hill, but as they reached the front gate, something very odd happened. The rainbow disappeared!

"We're too late!" sighed Cleo.

But Barney was not ready to give up yet. "The rainbow is gone," he said, "but maybe the pot of gold is still there. Where's my shovel?"

And before Cleo could stop him, the silly little bear was busy digging up his father's beloved tulip bed.

Just at that moment, Barney's father came out of the house. "Stop right there, young bear!" he called. He didn't sound happy.

But as he spoke, something shiny went *clink!* on Barney's shovel and came flying toward his father.

Mr Bear caught it in one large paw.

"Why, goodness me," he said, "it's the ring I lost when I was weeding last year!"

After that, Mr Bear didn't have the heart to be cross with Barney.

"Maybe rainbows do have gold at the end of them," he laughed. "Let me know when you see another one, Barney!"

Mother Bear's Problem

One morning, Mother Bear had a worried look on her furry face. "I know there's something I'm supposed to remember about today," she said, "but I can't for the life of me think what it is. I'm pretty sure it's something important."

"It's my birthday!" suggested Barney hopefully.

"Don't be silly," said his mother. "That's in October."

"It's *your* birthday!" Barney was trying to help.

"I think," said Mother Bear coldly, "I'd remember my own birthday, Barney. I may have forgotten one little thing, but I haven't completely lost my senses."

But Mother Bear was still worried. She checked her calendar to make sure that it wasn't time for her dentist's appointment, or Barney's school concert, or Mr Bear's fishing contest. She went through her papers to make sure that her bills were paid. She looked in the washing machine to see if there was laundry to be hung out or ironed. Still she knew that she had not remembered the thing she had forgotten.

"Never mind," said Mr Bear at lunchtime. "If we have nothing else to do this afternoon, let's watch that old film on television. We can put our feet up and relax."

By half-past three, Mother Bear and her husband were settled on the sofa with mugs of coffee, a box of chocolates, and wearing their oldest, comfiest slippers (which in Mr Bear's case were almost antiques!).

The film was so exciting that Mother Bear almost forgot about her problem, until . . . *Driiiiiiiing!* . . . there came a ring at the doorbell.

Mother Bear felt a sinking feeling in her tummy that had nothing to do with eating too many chocolates.

"Hello, darlings!" called Aunt Hortense, opening the door herself with a flourish. "I've come to stay until Monday as I promised," she said, from under her huge hat.

"I've remembered what I forgot," groaned Mother Bear to Mr Bear, too softly for Aunt Hortense to hear. "I was going to suggest that we all went away for the weekend!"

How Many Paws?

O ne fine day, several little bears and their
parents set off for a picnic at the beach. The
grown-up bears carried huge baskets of goodies,
while the little bears had almost as much to carry,
since they had brought every pail and shovel they
could find.

"Phew!" said Barney's father, when they
reached the beach at last. "You little bears can start
making sandcastles, while we get everything ready
for lunch."

But it was such a wonderful, sunny day that
almost all the grown-up bears had fallen fast asleep
before the little bears had really started on their
sandcastles.

"Look!" said Bettina, a very naughty little bear,
"while they are sleeping, we could have just a little
taste of the picnic."

Although most of the little bears were usually good little bears, that did sound like a very good idea. Barney peeked into the nearest basket, which had a missing strap, and saw a plastic box. With just a little twist of his paw, he managed to lift off the lid. Inside was a big chocolate cake!

One by one, the little bears squeezed their paws into the basket and took a taste of the cake. It was the yummiest cake they had ever tasted, and it somehow was even more delicious because they could only eat a tiny bit of it at one time.

It wasn't very long before all that was left of the cake was a pile of sticky crumbs.

"Quick!" said Bettina. "We'd better start making our sandcastles right now, or the grown-ups will wonder what we've been doing."

So when the grown-up bears awoke from their snooze a few minutes later, they found themselves surrounded by fine sandcastles. And not long after that, they found themselves missing one very fine chocolate cake.

"Oh dear," said Barney, shaking his head sadly. "I suppose it will be almost impossible to find out whether it was taken by seagulls or crabs or . . . er . . . turtles."

"Or bears!" said his father. "I'm happy to say that it will be very easy to find out who has eaten the cake, because the chocolate has made lots of sand stick to their paws and noses!"

The Star Bears

Late at night, when all his clocks were striking twelve, Mr Minim the clock mender loved to sit at his bedroom window and look at the stars. Nowadays, he found that he did not need as much sleep as he once did. Looking out at the little sparkling lights in the sky passed the time wonderfully.

Ever since he was a very young bear, Mr Minim had loved the night sky. His wise old grandfather had told him the names of all the groups of stars, and Mr Minim could still remember every one of them.

"I wish the young bears today were interested in astronomy," said Mr Minim to himself.

Next morning, Mrs Bear and Barney came into Mr Minim's shop. Mrs Bear had brought her best clock to be mended.

"It used to keep time beautifully," she said, "but last night it was almost midnight before Barney went upstairs to bed because the clock was wrong."

"Almost midnight?" said Mr Minim. "Then you must have seen the star bears."

"I did see the stars," said Barney, "but I didn't see any bears."

"That's because you didn't know where to look," said Mr Minim. "You need someone to show you – perhaps your daddy or Mrs Bear here."

"I'm afraid my husband and I wouldn't know where to look either," said Mrs Bear. "Perhaps you could come and show us one fine night."

"I'll bring your clock back tonight," said Mr Minim. "Will ten o'clock be all right?"

"Oh yes!" cried Barney, who loved to stay up late.

That night, Mr Minim showed the whole Bear family lots of interesting things about the night sky. Best of all, he showed them the star bears.

"There's the Great Bear," he said, "and there's the Little Bear."

"Is he older than me?" asked Barney.

"Young bear," laughed Mr Minim, "he's even older than *me*! And that really *is* old!"

31

The Lost Ribbon

In many ways, thought Cleo, Emmeline Bruin was the most annoying bear at school. All that Emmeline cared about was looking pretty. She wouldn't join in any rough games in case the frills on her dress got torn. She wouldn't play in the sand in case her paws got dirty. In fact, she was no fun at all.

"I'm never going to be good friends with Emmeline," Cleo told Barney one day on the way home from school. "She doesn't care about anyone but herself."

The very next day at school, all the little bears went on a nature walk with their teacher, Mr Tedson. They were supposed to be looking carefully at trees and picking up any leaves that had fallen to the ground.

"The shape of the leaf will tell you what kind of tree it has come from," said Mr Tedson.

But the little bears had not been in the woods for long before Emmeline began to wail.

"I've lost my ribbon!" she sobbed. "It was my best red ribbon!"

Cleo had always thought that Emmeline looked a little silly with a big bow between her ears, but with the other bears, she began hunting for the lost ribbon.

In fact, it was Cleo who found it first. At least, she was the first to see where it was. In a little bush beside the path, a tiny bird was busy weaving the ribbon into her nest. Cleo could see at once that pulling out the ribbon would destroy the nest.

Cleo was about to turn away, determined never to tell anyone what she had seen, when she heard a sound behind her. It was Emmeline! Cleo held her breath. That spoiled little bear was sure to make a fuss and demand her ribbon back.

But Emmeline was smiling. "Let's not say anything," she whispered. "It looks much prettier there than on my head!" And she smiled at Cleo.

Cleo smiled back. You can't always tell what someone is like just by looking at them, she thought. And she knew right there and then that she and Emmeline were going to be the very best of friends after all.

Cousin Carlotta

One morning, Mrs Bear got a letter. "It's an invitation," she said, "to a Grand Ball given by Mrs Carlotta Carmody. I've never heard of her!"

"You must know her," cried Mr Bear. "I've never been to a Grand Ball, and I'd like to go to this one."

"We can't go to a party given by someone we don't know," said Mrs Bear. "And the name doesn't sound familiar at all."

"Look, there's some writing on the back!" cried Barney, who had been peering up at the invitation.

Mrs Bear turned the invitation over. Scribbled on the back was a short message. "Dear Cousin, Yes, this is me, little Carly! I've married James Justin Jackson Carmody III. Do come to our party!"

"I don't believe it!" cried Mrs Bear. "Cousin Carly was the scruffiest, untidiest, and, quite honestly, the messiest bear I ever knew. The very idea of that harum-scarum bear in a ball gown is quite beyond me. But we shall have to go, of course."

"Oh, of course," smiled her husband.

Three weeks later, the Bear family, dressed in their finest clothes, arrived at Cousin Carlotta Carmody's mansion. It was huge!

"I feel faint," said Mrs Bear. "Barney, there will be no running about, no jumping, and definitely no sliding down stairs. Do you understand?"

"Yes," said Barney, looking regretfully at the wonderfully long and curving banisters.

All the guests were gathered in the hall, waiting for their hostess to make her grand entrance.

Suddenly, there was a chandelier-jingling yell.

"*Wheeeeeeeeeee!*" Cousin Carlotta made a grand entrance, all right – sliding down the banisters! Unfortunately, she left most of her train dangling from a picture frame, and her tiara was over one eye by the time she reached the bottom.

Mrs Bear forgot her nerves in a second. She ran forward to help her cousin to her feet.

"Carly," she smiled, "you haven't changed a bit!"

The Bear on the Stairs

The Bear family enjoyed Cousin Carlotta's party enormously, but they did not have much chance to look around her beautiful house – there was simply too much dancing and eating and talking to be done!

"Darlings, you must come back next week for a proper visit," said Carlotta, as the Bears left, well after midnight.

"We would be delighted," said Mrs Bear quickly. She adored looking around other people's homes.

Only Barney was not so sure that he wanted to go. He wasn't very interested in carpets and curtains.

The following Saturday, the Bear family arrived just before lunch. They had a splendid meal in the very fine dining room, then Mr and Mrs Bear set off with Carlotta for the Grand Tour.

"I think I'll stay here," said Barney, "and . . . er . . . look at the pictures."

Barney wandered around for a while, before going to sit on the grand staircase. He felt very bored and let out a big sigh.

"You could play with me, if you like," said a little bear on the stair above.

Barney jumped. He hadn't even noticed the bear, who was wearing strange clothes, made out of some shiny stuff. But he looked like a friendly little bear, and pretty soon Barney and the bear, who said that his name was Charles, were playing a wonderful game running up and down the hallway. Barney couldn't remember when he had had so much fun.

"There you are!" came his father's voice suddenly. "I hope you've been behaving yourself, Barney."

"Oh yes," said his son. "I've been playing with Ch…" and he turned to introduce his friend. But the little bear was nowhere to be seen.

Cousin Carlotta looked at Barney strangely. "What did the little bear look like?" she asked.

Barney hesitated, looking around for inspiration. Then, suddenly, he saw a large picture of Charles on the wall.

"That's him," he said. "That's my friend Charles."

Carlotta smiled. "That's my husband's great-great-great-grandfather," she said. "He lived over two hundred years ago – but he does like to make sure that young visitors feel at home!"

A Bear's Best Friend

One year, an uncle who lived overseas very unwisely gave Cleo a joke book for her birthday. It was dreadful. All day long, Cleo was trying out the jokes on her friends and family. And most of them were not very funny at all.

"What do you call a sleeping dinosaur?" she asked her father.

"I don't know, Cleo," groaned her long-suffering dad. "What do you call a sleeping dinosaur?"

"A brontosnorus!" chortled Cleo. "What goes clomp, clomp, clomp, clomp, clomp, clomp, clomp, squoosh?"

"I'll make you go squoosh, if you're not careful," grunted her father. "I don't know. What does go clomp, clomp, clomp, clomp, clomp, clomp, clomp, squoosh?"

"An octopus with one shoe off!" Cleo couldn't stop giggling. "What does Tarzan sing at Christmastime?"

"You're not still asking those awful jokes, are you, Cleo?" asked her mother, coming in at that moment. "I don't know. What does Tarzan sing at Christmastime?"

"Jungle bells! Jungle bells!" sang Cleo, waving her book in the air.

"Cleo! We didn't think they could get worse, but they have!" cried her parents together. "How many more pages are there?"

"Oh, hundreds!" laughed Cleo, looking at her book. "Who is a bear's best friend?"

Cleo's mother sank into a chair. "I don't know," she sighed wearily. "Who is a bear's best friend?"

Cleo turned the page, and gave a little cry. "Oh, they've forgotten to put in the answer!"

"That's fine, Cleo," replied her father, leaping out of his chair, "because for once I know the punch line to that joke. Who is a bear's best friend? It's the very sensible grown-up bear who takes away her joke book while some of her friends and family are still speaking to her!" And in two big strides, he'd grabbed the book and carried it away to his shed in the backyard.

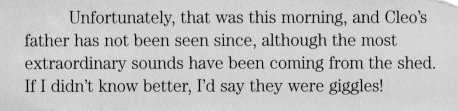

Unfortunately, that was this morning, and Cleo's father has not been seen since, although the most extraordinary sounds have been coming from the shed. If I didn't know better, I'd say they were giggles!

The Striped Scarf

One frosty afternoon, Mr Bear came in for lunch rubbing his paws. "It's so cold out there," he said, "I thought my ears would fall off."

Barney looked anxiously at his father's ears, but they looked fine.

"What I need," said Mr Bear carelessly, knowing that his birthday was just a few weeks away, "is a nice long scarf to wrap around my neck *and* my ears."

Just as carelessly, Mrs Bear asked her husband, "Is there any particular way that you would like the scarf to look?"

"Well, it should definitely be red," said Mr. Bear. "I've always looked good in red."

Over the next few days, Barney noticed that his mother's workbag was more bulging than usual, and just occasionally he caught sight of a tiny strand of red wool.

Mrs Bear was right on schedule until the day that Miss Bouquet in the flower shop complimented Mr Bear on the blue sweater he was wearing.

"You know," said Mr Bear later, "I think if I *were* to have a scarf, it should probably be blue."

Mrs Bear groaned. It was too late to start again. But Barney had a bright idea.

"What about stripes?" he suggested.

Well, that *was* a good idea, especially since, over the next few days, Mr Minim commented on how much he liked Mr Bear's yellow shirt, Mr Leaf asked where he could get a green tie just like Mr Bear's, and Barney, without thinking, asked if he could borrow his father's orange woolly hat. Mrs Bear made several trips to the wool shop, and her workbag was soon more bulging than ever.

On his birthday morning, Mr Bear felt a little anxious. What if his hints had gone unnoticed? He needn't have worried. Not only did he open the brightest scarf you have ever seen, but it was the longest, too!

"I think we're going to have to share this," laughed Mr Bear. "Look, it's long enough to wrap around the whole family!"

Paws with Patches

One day in a storybook, Cleo saw a picture of a bear with patches on his paws. She ran to her mother at once.

"Oh, please tell me, what has happened to this poor bear's paws? They've got bits and pieces sewn on all over them."

Her mother was busy working out her finances, but she glanced at the book and smiled.

"Oh, that's nothing to worry about. It's just a bear who has done a lot of work with his paws, so they have worn out. A kind friend has sewn some patches on for him. Now hurry along and set the table for me. I must add these figures up before we eat."

But Cleo didn't help her mother. She folded her arms and sat down in a chair.

A few minutes later, her mother looked up. "Will you do as I asked, Cleo, please?"

"No!" said Cleo.

The older bear could hardly believe her ears. Even Cleo's little brother looked up from where he was playing on the floor. Cleo was usually such a good little bear.

"Well, will you go and get your father?" Cleo's mother tried again.

"No," said Cleo.

And it was the same for the rest of that day, and that evening, and the next morning too. Cleo wouldn't pass things at the table. She refused to help wash the dishes. She wouldn't even help to bathe her little brother, which she usually loved. And in the morning, she wouldn't help with breakfast at all.

Cleo went to nursery school and came back with a note from the teacher to say that she had been difficult and quite unlike her usual self.

"Sit down, Cleo," said her mother. "We need to have a serious talk."

It wasn't very long before Cleo explained everything. "I just don't want my paws to wear out," she said, "so I'm saving them."

Cleo's mother laughed. "I'm surprised about that," she said, "considering how much most bears *want* patches on their paws."

"Do they?"

"Oh yes, it's like wearing a medal. It shows what a long and useful life you've led," explained her mother.

Well, ever since then, Cleo has been a *very* helpful little bear, though her paws look perfect to me!

The Singing Bear

If you walk along the main street of Bearborough at six o'clock in the morning, there is usually very little going on. On Wednesdays, of course, when there is a market, there may already be a few stallholders setting out their goods, but most of the week, Bearborough is a very quiet place.

And that is why it was so shocking when the singing began. Yes, singing. At about six o'clock, when most bears are still tucked up in their beds, a sound would ring out across the square.

TRA-la-la-la-la-la-la-LAAAAA!

It wasn't a horrible sound. In fact, it was quite a lovely sound. But it wasn't the kind of thing you expect to hear when your ears are still snuggled in your pillow.

The first morning that this happened, bears shook their heads and thought they were dreaming. But by the third morning, bears dressed in a strange assortment of nightclothes gathered in the street to try to stop the disturbance.

TRA-la-la-la-la-la-la-LAAAAA!

"It can't go on!" cried Mr Minim. "I need my sleep!"

44

"Tell me about it!" Mrs Cuddles had baby twins who were often hard to settle.

"But listen!" fashionable Albert held up his paw. "It's beautiful, isn't it?"

And sure enough, when everyone listened hard, they realized that it was the most glorious sound they had ever heard coming from the mouth of a bear.

TRA-la-la-la-la-la-la-LΛΛΛΛΛ! La-LA! La-LA!

Mr Leaf the librarian put his head out of his front door and cleared his throat.

"It's my sister," he said. "She's an opera singer. Her stage name is Ursula Pallas. You may have heard of her. She's staying with me for a week, and I'm afraid she has to rehearse."

Ursula Pallas? In Bearborough? *The* Ursula Pallas? The bears were stunned.

"O-o-of course she must be allowed to sing," stammered Mr Minim. "She's the greatest singer in the world."

Even Mrs Cuddles admitted this was true.

At that moment, one of Mr Leaf's windows was thrown open and a famous face appeared.

"Darlings!" cried La Pallas. "I will perform especially for you, here in the square, tonight at seven."

The concert is still talked of in Bearborough. And they say that if you are very quiet, you can still hear the great Pallas's extraordinary voice echoing softly around the square.

Bear Facts

Barney and Cleo were having supper at Barney's house. Cleo's mother had told her that she must try to think of interesting things to talk about, so that everyone would think she was a polite guest and would invite her again.

"Did you know, Mr Bear," Cleo began, "that bears are related to raccoons?"

"Raccoons?" replied Barney's father in surprise. "Oh, I don't think so, Cleo. They're very different from us."

"No, it's true," said Cleo politely. "I read about it in my Encyclopedia of Bears."

"Really?" Mr Bear usually liked to know best about everything, so he tried to think of something that Cleo might not know.

"Did you know that there are white bears who live on the ice all the time?" he asked.

"Oh, yes," said Cleo. "They're called polar bears and they live on fish. I had one as a penpal once, but his writing was a bit hard to read."

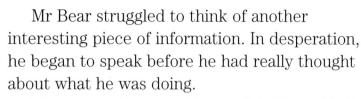

Mr Bear struggled to think of another interesting piece of information. In desperation, he began to speak before he had really thought about what he was doing.

"Of course, the rarest bear of all," he said, "is the green bear of Thailand. It is almost never seen because it can hide so easily in the trees."

"A green bear? There isn't anything about it in my encyclopedia," said Cleo.

Mr Bear felt that he had gone too far now to turn back.

"No," he said airily, "it is so rare that scientists are trying to keep it a secret. They don't want tourists going and disturbing it. I was lucky enough to see one on my travels, but I don't usually talk about it."

Mrs Bear coughed loudly at the other end of the table.

"Your travels, darling?" she said sweetly. "When was that?"

"Oh, long before I met you, honey," said Mr Bear, "when I was a young bear, you know."

"Cleo," said Mrs Bear, "I feel I should warn you that there are bear facts and then there are what are known as bear-faced lies. You can't believe everything you hear."

"Oh, don't worry Mrs Bear," said Cleo with dreadful honesty. "I don't believe everything that old bears say. After all, their brains go all mushy, don't they?"

"That's very true," laughed Mrs Bear, as her husband hurried off to hide his confusion.

The Flyaway Laundry

It was a beautiful windy day in Bearborough. Barney really wanted to go and fly his kite up on the hill behind the town, but his mother said that he mustn't go so far on his own, and she was too busy doing the laundry to go with him.

It wasn't like Barney to volunteer to help around the house, but he really wanted to fly his kite, so he made a suggestion. "If I help you with the laundry," he said, "will you come up on the hill with me this afternoon?"

Barney's mother smiled. "That's a good idea," she said, "and look, the first load has just come out of the machine. You can go outside and hang it out for me, while I put the next load in."

The washing basket was very full. It was all the little bear could do to carry it to the line, especially when he got outside and the wind began to push against him. At last, he reached the clothesline and put down the basket.

Oh dear, it wasn't easy! The wild wind tugged at the clothes before Barney could hang them out. And those clothes were really difficult to hold on to. First one of his father's socks went whirling away and over the fence. Then a T-shirt started flapping and flicking Barney on the nose. He held on as hard as he could, but still the T-shirt broke free and sailed away into the flower garden next door.

Just then, Barney's mother came out to see how he was doing.

"I'm sorry," gasped Barney, "but I just can't control this laundry!"

He had picked up one of his father's flashier shirts, and it too was struggling to get away.

"Hold on, Barney," cried his mother. "I'll hold on to the other sleeve!"

But as the two bears held on tight to the shirt, determined not to let it escape, the wind puffed into it like a sail and lifted them both off their paws!

"Don't let go, Barney!" cried his mother, as they sailed into the cabbage field on the other side of the fence.

"Whee!" called Barney. "This is better than flying my kite any day!"

The two bears landed with a bump in the field, still holding on to the shirt.

"I think it's too windy for laundry or kite-flying today," laughed Barney's mother, out of breath. "Let's have cocoa and cookies in front of the fire instead!"

Bears Ahoy!

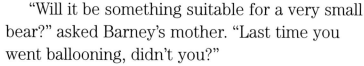

Ever since their first meeting on the bus home from Bearborough, Barney's granny and Bertram Bear (and his friendly mouse) had been great friends. They liked to take young Barney out and about with them, so the little bear was not surprised when Granny telephoned from Bertram's house to invite Barney on a mystery trip the next day.

"Will it be something suitable for a very small bear?" asked Barney's mother. "Last time you went ballooning, didn't you?"

Barney couldn't hear what Granny said, but it must have been reassuring, for he heard his mother agreeing that Barney could be called for at half past nine the next morning.

Barney was ready to go when the doorbell rang next day. As soon as he opened the door, he knew that he was in for an exciting day.

"Ahoy there, young bear!" called Granny and Bertram. They were dressed for a day on a boat and seemed determined to talk like old sea bears.

"Don't you worry, me hearty," said Bertram to Mrs Bear. "We'll bring him back shipshape and no mistake."

Barney was very excited as they walked down the hill. Were they going on a sailing ship? Or a steamer? Or even a fishing boat?

"There she is, the *Ellie May*," said Bertram proudly, as they reached the bridge over the river. "As neat a little craft as you ever did see."

Barney couldn't help feeling a little disappointed when he saw that the *Ellie May* was a very, very small boat!

But Bertram's enthusiasm was catching.

"All aboard," he cried. "We must sail on the next tide!"

"Aye, aye, Captain," called Barney. "Can I be first mate?"

"I'm afraid that job's already taken," said Bertram, winking at Granny, whose ears turned a little pink. "How would you like to be ship's cook?"

Bertram looked uncertain until Granny whispered that this meant being in charge of the sandwiches.

But I'm sorry to report that when they were a long way down the river and the Captain called for lunch, there didn't seem to be many sandwiches left. Barney and Bertram exchanged a long look of understanding.

"Pirates?" asked Bertram.

"Hundreds of 'em, Cap'n!" agreed Barney.

51

Are You There?

One wet afternoon, Cleo was very bored. She played with her train set (but some of the track seemed to be missing). She looked at her book about butterflies (but it just made her want to be outside). She bounced on her bed (until her mother stopped her).

"Can't you find something interesting to do?" said her mother, as she watched Cleo straightening her bed.

"No," said Cleo. "There isn't anything."

"Then you can play with your brother," her mother replied. "He's bored too."

Now Cleo loved her baby brother very much, but she had always thought he was much too small to play with. He couldn't do jigsaw puzzles or read books. Although he could crawl about very quickly, he was a little wobbly on his paws, so he wasn't any good at running and jumping games either.

Cleo looked cross. She was just about to say something not very nice about her brother when she saw him, sitting on the floor, peek out at her between his paws.

"*Boo!*" he said.

Cleo smiled. Maybe there was a game she could play with the baby after all. He put his paws over his face once again, and Cleo crept up close and whispered, "Are you there, baby bear?"

With a giggle, the little bear peeked between his paws.

"Yes," he said and crawled away.

Cleo thought the game was over, but her little brother pulled his mother's cardigan, which was on a chair, over his head.

"Are you there, baby bear?" called Cleo.

The mound of pink wool swayed from side to side, as if it was shaking its head.

"Oh yes you are!" Cleo whisked the cardigan away, and her brother collapsed into giggles.

Pretty soon, the baby realized that he could hide behind things as well as underneath them. This time, Cleo hid her eyes as he crawled away.

"Are you there, baby bear?" she called.

There was no reply. Cleo had to hunt around the room to find that little bear. As she went, she called, "Where, oh where is baby bear?" and soon found herself making up rhymes to amuse him.

"Where, oh where is baby bear?

Is he here behind the chair?"

It was fun. When the little bears' mother came to call them for supper, neither of them wanted to stop playing, and Cleo has loved her little brother even more from that day to this.

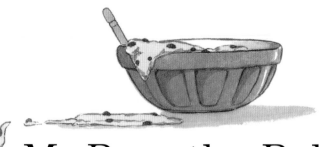

Mr Bear the Baker

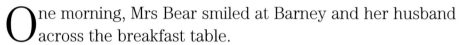

O ne morning, Mrs Bear smiled at Barney and her husband across the breakfast table.

"I'm going shopping with Granny today," she said. "We're both going to buy hats. I want you two boys to take care of the house and of each other."

"We'll be fine," said Mr Bear. "We've got things we need to do as well," he added mysteriously.

As soon as Mrs Bear had left the house, Barney's dad hurried him into the kitchen.

"It's your mother's birthday tomorrow," he said, "and I thought we could bake her a cake."

"Us?" asked Barney. "Are we any good at baking?"

"We're the best," said Mr Bear confidently. "Now we'll both put on these aprons."

Barney felt pretty silly in his apron, but he thought he didn't look as silly as his dad, so it must be fine.

After that, the bears had a wonderful time, weighing and measuring, stirring and mixing.

"I think that's about right," said Mr Bear, looking suspiciously at the rather odd-looking mixture. "It's time to put it in the oven."

Pretty soon, there was a delicious smell coming from the oven. At least, there was after Mr Bear remembered to turn it on.

"Time to clean up, Barney," he said. But somehow, both the bears got sidetracked. Mr Bear felt that he must show his son his egg-juggling routine. And Barney did a lot of useful experiments with flour. In the middle of the mayhem, they heard the front door open.

Barney and his father rushed into the hallway, shutting the kitchen door behind them.

"You can't go in there for a minute," said Mr Bear firmly to his wife. "We've been doing something extra secret."

Mrs Bear looked at the two bears in front of her.

"Not much of a secret when most of it is all over your fur," she said, "and if I pay attention to what my nose is telling me, I think it's time something extra secret came out of the oven."

It took Barney and his father the rest of the day to clean up the kitchen – but only ten minutes to help Mrs Bear eat a very strange-looking but delicious cake the next day!

The Bravest Bear

One sunny afternoon, Cleo and Barney were playing in Barney's backyard. It was a warm afternoon, so they were pleased when Mrs Bear brought them glasses of lemonade to drink under the shade of the trees.

As they sat with their cool drinks, Cleo looked up at the branches above.

"Are you afraid of heights, Barney?" she asked.

"Of course not," said Barney. "I can climb ever so high. I'll show you if you like."

And before Cleo could stop him, young Barney was halfway up the tree, sitting on his own special branch.

"Come on up!" he called.

"No, no," said Cleo quickly. "You come down."

"You're not frightened, are you?" asked Barney. "All bears can climb trees. Everyone knows that. Are you a scaredy-bear, Cleo? Scaredy-bear! Scaredy-bear!"

Barney didn't mean to be horrible, but he was so used to finding that Cleo was better at things than he was that he was glad to be able to tease her about something.

Barney made such a fuss about Cleo's climbing that at last she couldn't bear it any longer.

"All right!" she said. "Just watch me!" And she started to climb the tree.

At first it was fine, but as soon as Cleo looked down from the lowest big branch, she began to shiver and shake.

"I don't like it, Barney," she said. "I really am afraid of heights and I want to get down. Will you help me, please?"

"You really are a scaredy-bear!" began Barney. "I'm much braver than you are! Ha ha!"

"I don't think so, Barney," said Mrs Bear, who had come out to get the empty lemonade glasses. "It took much more courage for Cleo to admit she was afraid than it did for you to climb a tree you have climbed lots of times before."

Barney knew she was right and quickly helped his friend to the ground. Cleo was soon her old self.

"Let's go and hunt for spiders," she said, not noticing that Barney was looking very worried indeed.

The Park Puzzle

One day, the whole Bear family decided to have a picnic in the park. Mr and Mrs Bear were there with Barney, and Granny had brought Bertram along. But after they had enjoyed a picnic of delicious food, all the grown-ups (and Bertram's mouse) fell asleep in the sunshine, and Barney was very bored.

He tried tossing daisies into his father's hat, but had to pretend to be asleep himself when one of them missed and landed on Mr Bear's nose.

He spent a little time on the swings, but they made him feel a bit sick after such a big lunch.

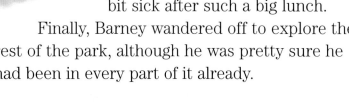

Finally, Barney wandered off to explore the rest of the park, although he was pretty sure he had been in every part of it already.

But Barney was wrong. Behind some bushes near the tennis courts, he found a little cabin. It was newly painted and had pots of flowers outside. Who could it belong to?

Barney tried the door, but it was locked. He stood on tip-paws and peered into the window, but he couldn't see a thing.

Barney puzzled about the mystery as he walked back to his family. They were all still asleep, except for Bertram, who was decorating Granny's hat with the daisies Barney had picked earlier.

"You look worried," said Bertram, as Barney approached.

"Not worried," said Barney, "just wondering." And he told Bertram all about the little cabin.

"That will be the caretaker's cabin," said Bertram. "The caretaker is an old friend of mine, and I'm pretty sure I know what he'll be doing in there on an afternoon like this. Come with me."

Barney followed Bertram back to the cabin, and Bertram lifted him up to the window. Yes, there was the caretaker, looking as comfortable as can be, and doing just what Barney's family was doing back on the grass.

"I'll never understand grown-up bears," sighed Barney.

59

Please, Dad!

When Cleo and her family set off for a weekend away, their little car was packed to the roof with all the things that simply couldn't be left behind. After Cleo's dad's fishing equipment, Cleo's little brother's things and almost all Cleo's toys had been fitted in, Cleo's mother suddenly realized that no one had packed any clothes. Everything had to be taken out and fitted in again, which took all morning.

Even so, there was hardly any room for the bears themselves when it was time to set off. And by then, tempers had become so frayed that Cleo's mother looked grim as she drove down the lane, and her husband looked desperate as he struggled to stop an enormous map from flapping into her face. To be fair, Cleo didn't help at all.

"Please, Dad," she said, when they had been going for ten minutes, "are we there yet?"

"We won't be there until very late at this rate, especially if we go the wrong way," her mother replied between clenched teeth. Her husband was now so entangled with the map that he couldn't speak.

Cleo waited five minutes. "Please, Dad, can we stop?"

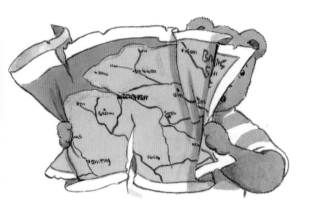

"Not already, Cleo, surely?" Her mother didn't sound very pleased, but she pulled over anyway. She didn't want accidents of *any* kind in her car!

They hadn't been back on the road for more than a minute or two when Cleo piped up again.

"Please, Dad, I think I've forgotten something."

"We haven't forgotten anything," said her mother, "except perhaps how to get there." For Cleo's Dad was flapping the map around in a worrying way.

"Please, Dad," Cleo began.

"If I hear one more word from you," said her mother grimly, "we'll go straight home. Is it right or left here?"

Turning first this way and then that, the family went on for another half hour.

"Please, Dad," said Cleo, "isn't that…?"

Both parents opened their mouths to tell her to be quiet, but the words never came. At the same moment they recognized that they were driving along the familiar lane to their own house. They had been going in a circle.

"Please, Dad," laughed Cleo. "I'm so glad to be home!"

Bertram's Books

O ne day, Bertram Bear announced that he was going to have a grand clear-out of his house.

"I've got far too much rubbish, collected over the years," he said. "There's hardly room for me in my house, never mind anyone else." And he smiled at Barney's granny.

"Can I help you?" asked Barney. "I'm really good at clearing things out, aren't I, Dad?"

"Last time I let you help me clear out my shed," said his father, "I couldn't find anything for weeks. But if Bertram is willing to take the risk, that's his business."

"Oh, I think we can find something for a small bear to do," said Bertram kindly.

When Barney and Granny arrived at Bertram's house, they soon realized how big the problem was. It looked as though Bertram had never thrown anything away in his life. There were newspapers and boxes everywhere, but most of all there were books on every table and chair and piled up all over the floor.

"I can't resist buying them," said Bertram. "I just love books, you see."

"I quite understand, but why not donate them to the library after you have read them?" suggested Granny. "I'm sure Mr Leaf would be very grateful."

"How clever you are, my dear, as always," said Bertram.

All afternoon, the bears carried books out to the front of the house, so that the library van could pick them up later.

As Bertram and Granny sat down for a rest, they looked around for Barney. The little bear was nowhere to be seen.

After two hours of frantic searching, Granny was very worried indeed. But just then the van arrived from the library.

"Has anyone lost a small bear?" asked the driver, as he lifted some books from the huge pile.

There was Barney, hidden in a little house of books and enjoying an exciting storybook so much that he hadn't even noticed he had been walled in with books.

"I've heard of bookworms," laughed Bertram, "but it looks as though you and I are both bookbears, young Barney."

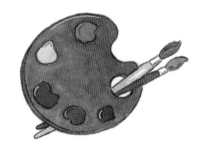

The Masterpiece

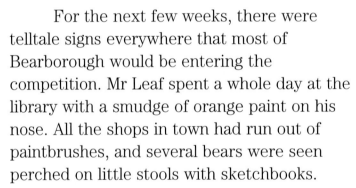

News soon spread around Bearborough that there was to be an Art Show. All bears had to do was send in their pictures. At the end of the show, the best grown-up picture and the best picture by a little bear would receive a prize.

For the next few weeks, there were telltale signs everywhere that most of Bearborough would be entering the competition. Mr Leaf spent a whole day at the library with a smudge of orange paint on his nose. All the shops in town had run out of paintbrushes, and several bears were seen perched on little stools with sketchbooks.

Of course, Barney, Cleo, and their families were all eager to enter the competition. Mr Bear was particularly anxious to win, but he found it very difficult to find the peace and quiet he needed, he said, for his talent to flourish. When Barney had left pawprints on his fourth sketch (completely by accident, of course), Mr Bear declared that the shed was the only place he could concentrate properly.

"My work will be very modern," he said, "but I'm sure that is what the judges will be looking for."

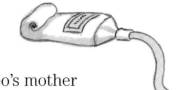

On the day that the pictures had to be submitted, Cleo's mother agreed to take all of them, from both families, in her car. Each picture was framed and wrapped in brown paper, with a label giving the age of the painter. Painters' names were written on the backs of the pictures.

Cleo's mother lay the pictures carefully on the back seat next to Cleo's baby brother's car seat. You can imagine how horrified she was when she arrived to find that the baby bear had spent the whole journey carefully pulling off the labels.

The harassed mother stuck them all back on as well as she could and carried them quickly into the show before anything else could happen to them.

On the last day of the show, everyone hurried to see what the judges had decided. Mrs Bear went in first with Barney while her husband parked the car.

"Congratulations, sweetheart!" she called when he arrived at last. "You've won first prize!"

Mr Bear's face lit up with pride, until his wife went on: "in the little bears' competition!"

Baby Bears

Barney didn't have any brothers and sisters, and he was sorry about that. When he saw Cleo playing with her baby brother, he thought what fun it must be. It made Cleo seem so grown-up and smart. Barney wanted to feel like that too.

"Couldn't we have a baby bear in our family?" he asked his mother one day.

Mr Bear, who was reading his paper by the fire, overheard Barney's question.

"One little bear is quite enough in this house, rampaging across my vegetable beds and leaving muddy pawprints on the carpet," he laughed, referring to a recent unfortunate incident when Barney had been pretending to be an explorer crossing strange lands.

"Baby bears don't rampage," said Barney. "I was only thinking of a little, tiny baby bear."

"But little bears get bigger," smiled his mother. "Look at the wall where we've measured you from time to time!"

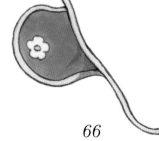

Still, Barney did think it might be better to be part of a bigger family. He decided to go and see Cleo to ask her what she thought.

But when Barney reached Cleo's house, the noise was incredible. Not one, not two, but ten baby bears were crawling and crying and getting up to all sorts of mischief on Cleo's living room carpet, while their parents sat around the table and tried not to notice what was going on.

"It's our turn to have the toddlers' group here," Cleo explained above the noise. "It only happens about twice a year, thank goodness!"

Barney looked down to find that one baby bear had dribbled on his paws, while another was busy trying to climb up his legs. Meanwhile, a third baby had managed to climb into a chair and was preparing to dive off onto the floor.

Barney rushed to save the diving baby, who screamed so loudly when she was picked up that Barney almost dropped her in fright. As he put her gently on the floor, he was just in time to save another baby from eating the leaves of a potted plant.

"Thank you for coming along to help, Barney," said Cleo's mother. "It means that we grown-up bears can have a little rest."

It was Barney who needed a rest when he staggered home an hour later.

"Let's not have any more baby bears," he told his amused parents. "One rampaging little bear in this house is quite enough!"

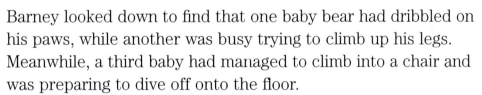

The Very Best Bear

Granny Bear need not have worried. When Barney brought her breakfast in bed (and managed not to spill a single drop) on her wedding morning, the sun was shining and there wasn't a cloud in the sky.

Much to Mrs Bear's amazement, everything was right on schedule. Granny's flowers arrived on time, and Barney managed to get dressed *and* put on his bow tie without any mishaps. Even Mr Bear was ready as the special car drew up at the front door.

But just as the Bear family was leaving the house, the telephone rang. Granny looked concerned, as Barney's mother hurried to answer it.

"Don't worry, we'll think of something," the others heard her say, as she put the phone down.

In the car, Mrs Bear explained that Bertram's best bear's car had broken down, and he wouldn't be able to make it in time for the wedding.

"What's a best bear?" asked Barney.

"It's a special friend of the bridegroom," explained his father. "My best bear was Uncle George."

"Maybe you could be the best bear, Dad," said Barney.

"Well, that's really for Bertram to decide," replied his father. "But anyway, I've already got a job. I'm giving Granny away."

Barney thought that was pretty funny, until his parents explained that it was just a way of showing that Granny was going to be part of a new family with Bertram.

Bertram was waiting on the steps, as the Bear family arrived. And he didn't look worried at all.

"You seem to have solved your problem," said Mr Bear.

"I have now," said Bertram. "I've decided to ask the bear who brought Martha and me together to be our best bear. And I couldn't think of a better bear to do it, so he really *is* the best. Come on, Barney, it's time to go!"

So Granny's happiest day was Barney's proudest day, too, and most of their friends from Bearborough were there to make sure that it certainly was a day to remember.

Five-Minute
Farmyard
Tales

Welcome to Windytop Farm!

There's always something happening down on the
farm when these friends get together!

Farmer Barnes   Annie   Harold

Duchess

Pompom

Delilah

Cackle

Biggy Pig

Lala Lamb

Busy Hen

Denby Dog   Pup

Dymphna   Mrs Speckles

Contents

Sweet Dreams, Harold!

When you have a warm, dry stable, filled with fresh, golden straw, and your tummy is full of oats and carrots and other good things, you should be able to get a good night's sleep – if you're a horse, of course! But poor old Harold, who had lived on Windytop Farm for a very long time, now spent all *day* dozing in the sun.

"It's because he's getting old," whispered Cackle the rooster. But a rooster's whisper, as you may know, is not very quiet. Old Harold raised his sleepy head and said, "No, it's not, Cackle. It's because I can't get a wink of sleep at night"

"Why not?" asked Busy Hen. "You've got a lovely stable. It's much nicer than our henhouse. I've often told Cackle."

"It's not that," yawned Harold. "It's the noise at night. It's terrible!"

Cackle started to strut about. "I do *not* make a noise in the night," he crowed. "I wait until it's almost, almost daybreak. I do! I do!"

"Nobody said it was you, Cackle," clucked Busy Hen. "Your crowing is beautiful. I believe it's those mice. Am I right, Harold?"

"Quite right," agreed the old horse. "They are scritch-scratching all night long. Some noises can be ignored – like the wind in the trees, or the rain on the roof. But you can't ignore scritch-scratching. You just can't."

"Leave it to me," said Busy Hen. And later in the day she went to Harold's stable and had a very long conversation with a little person with a twitchety nose and a long tail.

A week later, Harold was trotting about the farmyard as usual, much to everyone's delight. And Busy Hen was as proud as punch of the brand new henhouse she shared with Cackle and the other hens.

"I knew Farmer Barnes wouldn't leave us in that old henhouse once it had mice in it," she clucked. "And those mice just love their new home – so everyone's happy!"

The Cluckety Duck

Farmer Barnes' duckpond was never a very peaceful place. Hardly a day went by when there was not some kind of squawking and squabbling among the reeds. Those ducks were always making a noise. Sometimes it was because Carter Cat was prowling too close to their nests on the bank. Sometimes it was because Dymphna, their leader, had eaten almost all the lovely slimy weed at one end of the pond. Sometimes it was just because ducks love to hear the sound of their own voices.

One day, Farmer Barnes brought a new duck to the pond.

"Be nice to her, you daffy ducks," he said. "She's lived all by herself with an old lady for a long, long time. She's not used to your quacky, splashy ways."

For several days, the little duck paddled shyly round the pond and didn't say a word. The other ducks, who did their best to be kind, thought she must be shy. At last Dymphna, who was curious about the newcomer, waddled up and asked her how she was finding her new home.

The duck looked up and opened her beak. She said her first word on Windytop Farm. It was … *"Cluck!"*

For a moment, Dymphna thought her ears must be full of pond mud. But the little duck spoke again. "Cluck!" she said. "Cluck, cluckety, cluck!"

Dymphna was so surprised that she sat down *plop!* on her newly curled tail feathers. Whoever heard of a clucking duck? And the trouble was that none of the ducks could understand a word she clucked.

Dymphna knew that she would have to talk to Busy Hen. It was well known that Busy Hen knew several foreign languages, but Dymphna and Busy Hen were not the best of friends.

Later that day, the farmyard animals saw Busy Hen deep in conversation with the newcomer, fluffing her feathers and chatting as if they had been friends for years.

"It's quite simple," she told Dymphna that evening. "This little duck is an orphan. She was brought up by an old lady's French hen. So of course, she has never learned to speak duck language. We will have to teach her."

The new duck, whose name was Dolores, was a very quick pupil. How proud of her Dymphna and Busy Hen were when she first dived into the pond with a loud, "QUACK!"

I'm afraid the duckpond is noisier than ever these days!

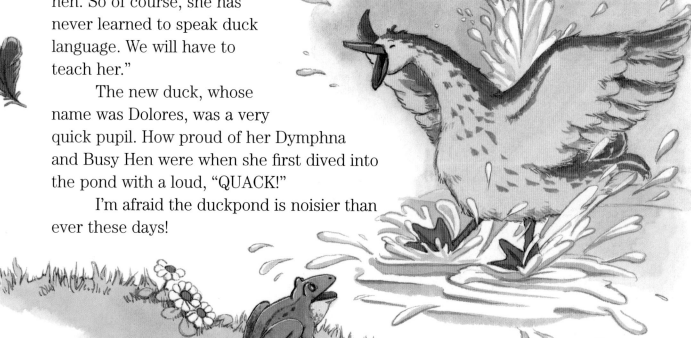

Biggy Pig's Problem

Biggy Pig was the oldest pig on Windytop Farm and he was also the biggest. That, of course, was how he got his nickname, for his real name was Brewster Barnstaple Buddleham Pride. Somehow, Biggy Pig sounded a lot more friendly, and Biggy was certainly a friendly pig.

One day, Farmer Barnes leaned over Biggy Pig's sty and scratched his back with a stick.

"Old friend," he said, "there's a very important day coming up for you on Friday. I want you to eat as much as you can, so that you're as big and fat as can be."

Although Biggy Pig snorted happily at Farmer Barnes, he was rather quiet for the rest of the day.

"What's the trouble, Biggy?" asked Harold the horse. "You seem to be off your fodder, old friend."

Biggy gulped. "I'm very much afraid," he said, "that I won't need fodder where I'm going. Farmer Barnes wants me to look as big and fat as I can for Friday. I think he means to take me to the market."

Harold looked serious. "That's terrible, Biggy," he said. "There's only one thing you can do. Diet! No one takes a thin pig to market."

So for the next few days, Biggy hardly touched his food. And Farmer Barnes was worried about him. But still, when Friday came, he loaded Biggy up into the trailer and set off for town.

"Farewell, old friends!" called Biggy, with a lump in his throat, as the farmyard animals lined up to wave goodbye.

But Biggy was in for a surprise. Farmer Barnes didn't take him to the market at all. He took him to the County Show, where Biggy Pig, in spite of his diet, looked as fat and handsome as any pig you have ever met. You should have seen how proud he looked as he arrived back at the farm – with his First Prize ribbon!

Where's That Goat?

Scraggles the goat had lived on Windytop Farm almost as long as Biggy Pig. But unlike Biggy, he was not popular with the other animals. The fact was you just couldn't trust Scraggles. Even if he *knew* he had found your best straw hat or your special store of apples, he would still eat them. He just couldn't help himself. To a goat, almost everything looks like food. In fact, almost everything *is* food.

"I wouldn't mind," said Harold the horse, "but that was my very best bridle – the one I wear for giving children rides at the local show. And it was so tough and chewy, I can't believe he enjoyed it."

"That's the trouble with goats," said Biggy Pig. "They've got such enormous appetites." (Although Biggy Pig could eat for a week without stopping, he did draw the line at hats and bridles.)

"Isn't there something we can do?" clucked Busy Hen. "I can't bear to lose another lovely nest of straw. Isn't there something we can do to stop that wretched goat?"

"No, my dear," crowed Cackle the rooster. "I'm afraid goats will be goats." And that really was the wisest thing that Cackle, who was not known for his brains, had ever said.

But as things turned out, the animals didn't have to do anything. Scraggles did it all by himself. One breezy morning, when the sun was shining, he took a liking to Farmer Barnes' laundry, flapping and flipping in the wind. He munched through three pairs of socks, the bottom half of a pair of pyjamas, half a shirt, two pillowcases, and several pairs of … well, *underwear.* He was just starting to nibble a delicious-looking vest, when Farmer Barnes came back to the farmhouse for his lunch.

Oh dear! There was roaring and raging, shouting and stamping. And Farmer Barnes went straight to his workshop to find a stout chain and an even stouter stake.

Now Scraggles has to content himself with a fresh patch of grass every day. And the cow called Duchess has a brand new hat with no bites out of it at all.

Busy Hen's Chicks

One spring day, Busy Hen sat down on her nest and stayed there. She didn't get up to scratch in the dust, or cluck at Dymphna Duck, or tell everyone on the farm just what she thought about any subject that came into her head. No, she simply sat.

Of course, all the animals knew what *that* meant. Busy Hen was going to hatch out some chicks, as she did every year at this season.

"How many will it be this time, Busy Hen?" called Harold the horse as he clip-clopped by on his way to the meadow.

Busy Hen put her head under her feathers and counted. "Ten and then some more," she said at last. Hens are not very good at counting, although they are excellent with foreign languages.

Even for Busy Hen, that was a lot of eggs, but she was determined to hatch out every one of them, one day soon.

And sure enough, the morning came when Busy Hen heard a tap-tap-tapping from under her feathers. Pretty soon, the sweetest little chick you've ever seen popped his head out of his egg. Before long, his twelve little brothers and sisters popped their heads out too. Busy Hen cuddled them close under her wings and smiled. She didn't sleep a wink all night, as she guarded her precious babies.

But next morning, the little chicks became restless. First one and then another popped out from under Busy Hen's feathers and wobbled off on spindly legs to explore the world.

"Help!" called Busy Hen. She didn't know what to do. Thirteen chicks were just too many. If she ran after one of them, another two escaped in the opposite direction. If she kept five of them warm under her wings, the other eight wandered out of the henhouse and got their feet cold.

It wasn't until Biggy Pig suggested a babysitting service that Busy Hen heaved a sigh of relief. Each little chick found itself with an extra special aunt or uncle.

"How about your usual six chicks next year, Busy Hen?" suggested Harold, as he puffed after his special nephew.

But Busy Hen smiled to herself and put up her scrawny feet. As everyone knew, numbers were not her strong point…

83

Little Lala Lamb

When the snow was lying thick on the ground at Windytop Farm, Farmer Barnes set off to find his sheep.

The snow had come just when he was expecting the sheep to start having their lambs, and he was afraid the little ones would not survive the bitter cold.

You can imagine how relieved he was to find the sheep sheltering behind a wall. And none of them had yet had their lambs.

"Come on, my old dears," said the farmer. "You come with me to my warm barn. It's too cold for you out here."

But when the farmer had shepherded all the woolly animals into his biggest barn, he counted them to make sure they were all there. They weren't. One sheep was missing.

Farmer Barnes turned his coat collar up and went out into the cold one more time. Snow was flying all around him, and he could hardly see where he was going.

Out on the hill once more, the farmer searched behind every sheltering wall and under every bare-branched tree. He was cold and hungry, but still he searched on.

At last, just as he thought he would have to turn back, he heard, above the wind, a little sound. He stood very still and listened. It sounded – yes, it really did – it sounded like someone singing, right by his feet!

Farmer Barnes bent down and began to dig with his bare hands. Just below the surface he came upon two bright little eyes – and then two more! The missing sheep had had her lamb, and it was the little lamb who was singing, buried in the snow.

The happy farmer tucked the lamb into his coat and helped her mother up. Then the three set off, back to the farmyard.

"I'm going to call you Lala," Farmer Barnes told the warm little lamb under his coat. "Because if you hadn't sung your lala song, you and your mother might never have come safely home."

Farmer Barnes' Apple Pie

One summer, Farmer Barnes bought a pair of geese. They were beautiful white birds who honked when anyone came near them.

"There have been a lot of burglaries around here," the farmer told them. "Your job is to warn me if any strangers come to Windytop Farm. In return, you can run about in my lovely orchard all day long."

The geese honked as if they understood, and Farmer Barnes went happily back to his work.

And the geese proved their worth much sooner than Farmer Barnes could have imagined. The very next day, when the farmer was away cutting barley, two men drove into the farmyard in a battered old truck.

They skulked around the farmyard for a while, checking that no one was about, then they hurried over to the pigsty and started scooping up the new little piglets.

Of course, the piglets squealed, but that was nothing to the noise the geese made in the nearby orchard. They honked and spread their wings. And they ran so quickly towards the rickety fence that they broke right through it and came rushing into the farmyard, where the men were just loading the last little piglet into the back of their truck.

But at the sight of the geese, the men dropped the last piglet and ran for their lives. The first goose just had time to bite a big hole in the second man's trousers before the truck rumbled into life and revved out of the farmyard with the piglets tumbling one by one out of the open back doors.

Farmer Barnes had heard the commotion even from the other side of the farm. He was very, very pleased as he put the piglets back in their sty and mended the rickety fence.

But when autumn came, and the orchard was full of beautiful apples, Farmer Barnes found that he had a problem. Those geese were used to their orchard and wouldn't let him in! If he so much as approached the gate, they hissed and honked and spread their wings menacingly.

Farmer Barnes was a fair man. "Okay," he said, "you keep my farm safe night and day. I reckon you deserve some rosy apples, and I can go without my apple pie – this time!"

Duchess and Delilah

When the farm animals saw Duchess the cow with a pretty young calf by her side one morning, they were surprised.

"I didn't know she was expecting a *baby*!" hissed Dymphna to the other ducks. When Duchess was going to have a baby she looked as round and rolling as a barrel. No one had noticed any difference in the cow's trim figure. It was very strange.

Even more strange was the way Duchess treated her calf. She did her best to ignore it. Usually, she was the first to show off her new offspring to the whole farmyard. This time she was very off-hand about the whole thing.

"Oh that," she said to Busy Hen, when she clucked an inquiry. "Yes, she is a pretty calf, I guess, though her feet are big."

"So she *is* your calf?" asked Busy Hen, determined to get to the bottom of the matter.

"You could say that," said Duchess carelessly.

It took over a week for the story to come out. The calf came from a nearby farm, and Farmer Barnes had agreed to look after her.

"Duchess," he had said to his most motherly cow, "this little calf's mamma can't look after her, so I want you to do it. You'll take care of her so well."

Duchess did try to be kind to the little calf. She made sure she had sweet milk to drink and the warmest place in the cowshed to sleep. But somehow Duchess just couldn't warm to her new daughter.

"I can't forget that she isn't really my own calf," she confessed to Busy Hen, "and I'm not really her mother. What's more, she's called Delilah. Such a silly name!"

The little calf turned out to be very adventurous. Duchess found she had to spend more and more time rescuing her from difficult situations. And Duchess grumbled to all the animals, until they were really fed up.

Then, one day, the little calf got into real trouble. There was a commotion from the duck pond and a frightened cry from the calf. She had fallen into the water, but she hadn't learned to swim! Oh, no!

While all the animals were wondering what to do, Duchess plunged into action. She strode into the pond, grabbed the little calf by her tail, and hauled her out of the water. She was beaming with happiness as she licked the calf's face dry.

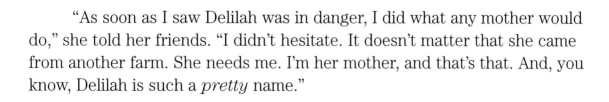

"As soon as I saw Delilah was in danger, I did what any mother would do," she told her friends. "I didn't hesitate. It doesn't matter that she came from another farm. She needs me. I'm her mother, and that's that. And, you know, Delilah is such a *pretty* name."

A Stitch in Time

Busy Hen was not usually afraid to speak her mind, but there were some subjects that even she felt were a little delicate. She confided in her best friend, Mrs Speckles.

"Surely someone else has noticed?" she clucked. "I don't like to say anything, but really something should be done."

"My dear, to what do you refer?" asked Mrs Speckles, leaning a little closer. She liked to speak in what she thought was a fancy way, which always annoyed Busy Hen.

"If you haven't noticed, I'm not sure I can tell you," clucked that lady, carelessly pecking at a piece of straw.

"Busy Hen!" cried Mrs Speckles, dropping her fancy voice in her eagerness to find out what the mystery was. "We've been friends for umpteen years. If you can't tell *me*, who can you tell?"

Busy Hen knew she was right. "It's Farmer Barnes," she said, without any more delay. "Or rather … it's Farmer Barnes' *trousers*!"

"Aaah," said Mrs Speckles wisely. She knew exactly what Busy Hen was talking about now. Earlier in the week, Farmer Barnes had torn the seat of his trousers on some brambles, and ever since, although he seemed not to notice, you could see a large portion of his underwear!

"You're quite right, my dear," said Mrs Speckles. "And I can guess what you're thinking. If you and I and some of the other ladies paid Farmer Barnes a little visit one night…?"

"Exactly," agreed Busy Hen. "How about tonight?"

And that is why, late that night, while Farmer Barnes snored in his bed, Busy Hen and Mrs Speckles and some of their friends hopped in through the window and got to work with needles, thread, and a piece of Harold's oldest blanket.

Next morning, Farmer Barnes appeared in his repaired trousers in all their glory. But he seemed to notice the patch no more than he had the hole!

"Ladies," said Busy Hen, "we did a fine job, but dear old Farmer Barnes needs a wife. I'm surer of it every day."

The other hens clucked their agreement, and I'm afraid, when Busy Hen makes up her mind about something, it is almost sure to happen!

Harold Saves the Day

Some of the smaller animals were covering their ears on Windytop Farm. Farmer Barnes was red in the face and shouting – and some of his language really wasn't fit for little ears to hear.

Everyone knew their dear old farmer wasn't really furious with his old tractor, even if he did give it a kick with his boot from time to time. He was just annoyed that he couldn't set off to work the bottom field as he had planned. The tractor just wouldn't start.

The animals knew that the tractor was ancient and that Farmer Barnes only kept it because he was fond of it. He could remember his father teaching him to drive it when he was a boy.

"He has that brand new shiny one," crowed Cackle to Biggy Pig. "Why can't he use that?"

Biggy Pig sighed. "Because, Cackle," he said, "the old tractor is standing right in front of the barn so the new tractor can't get out. Anyone can see that."

"Can't he push it out of the way?" asked Cackle.

"You try," suggested Biggy Pig. And I'm afraid that Cackle really has no brains at all, because he did!

When Farmer Barnes had shooed Cackle, who was also very red in the face now, away, he stomped into the house to call the mechanic. The animals could hear his conversation through the open door.

"What? *What?* Not until tomorrow? That's ridiculous! Oh, okay, I understand. See you then."

Poor Farmer Barnes came out of the house and looked hopelessly at the tractor. He sat down on the doorstep and buried his head in his hands. Just then, he heard a friendly clip-clopping noise. It was Harold.

The farmer looked up as the old horse nuzzled the top of his head with his nose. All at once, a smile came over the farmer's face.

"Harold!" he cried. "How do you feel like some work? Like in the old days?"

In no time, the farmer had harnessed Harold to the old tractor. Then he stood by his head and whispered a few encouraging words as Harold began to pull.

Cackle was so impressed by Harold's strength that he fell off his perch. And as the tractor rolled out of the way, *everyone* cheered.

The Paint Problem

O ne fine, still day, Farmer Barnes decided to do something he had put off for a long time. There was always so much to do on the farm he never had time to pay attention to the farmhouse. Now the paintwork was looking very shabby. It was time to give the doors and windows a new lick of paint.

Unfortunately, Farmer Barnes was not a man who enjoyed spending money. "Waste not, want not," was his motto. Did he go down to the store in town to buy a couple of large tins of paint? No, he did not. He went into his old workshop behind the henhouse and rummaged about until he found eleven – yes, eleven – cans of old paint. There was some red, some orange, a brilliant turquoise, white, a lot of green, some black, a tiny bit of silver, a pale yellow, two tins of dark brown, and a very vivid violet.

"He can't really be thinking of using all of them," hissed Biggy Pig to Cackle. "It's going to look *awful!*"

"All he's worried about," said Dymphna the duck, "is whether it will keep the wet out. Honestly! As if a little wet ever hurt anyone!"

Meanwhile, Farmer Barnes was scratching his head over the paint cans. He couldn't decide which to start with. It was just at this moment that Annie, who came to collect the eggs, drove into the farmyard. She was a comfortable-looking lady with hair that never seemed to stay where it was put and clothes that looked almost as old as Farmer Barnes'.

"Afternoon, Fred," she called. "What are you doing?"

Farmer Barnes pointed to the paints and explained the problem.

Now even Annie could see that it was not a good idea to paint a house using ten different paints. As was her way, she told Farmer Barnes exactly what she thought about the matter. And she told him straight. By the time she drove out of the yard with the eggs, Farmer Barnes was feeling pretty foolish. How everyone would have laughed at him if he had really painted his house like a rainbow! Still … the paint was too good to waste.

It was then that the farmer had his brilliant idea. He fetched one of Biggy's old water troughs and poured every drop of paint into it. Then he stirred it together with a big stick. There was plenty of paint for all the woodwork on the house. And it was all the same – a sludgy, muddy shade of brown.

When the house was painted, the animals shuddered in horror. It looked terrible. But Dymphna sighed a sigh of pure happiness. "Beautiful," she said. "As I always say, you can't beat mud, can you?"

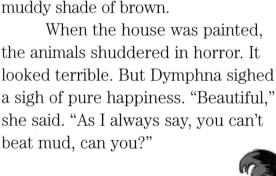

Windy Windytop

There's a reason why Windytop Farm is called Windytop Farm. Most of it is on top of a hill, for one thing, and it's very, very windy for another. Farmer Barnes had been careful to place all the animals' homes so that their doorways pointed away from the wind. But even so, sheds and stables always seem to have little chinks and crannies where the wind can whistle through. And you can always rely on the wind to find them.

One windy day, when Cackle had been blown off his perch on the henhouse roof for the fourth time, Duchess the cow called the animals together for a serious talk.

"This wind is getting worse," she said. "I can't remember it ever being as bad as this when I was young. I put it down to the windmills."

"What windmills?" asked Biggy Pig. "There are no windmills." He sometimes felt that Duchess was talking in riddles.

"Exactly!" cried Duchess eagerly. "In the old days there were windmills to use up the wind. Now it can just blow free."

There was silence for a moment, while everyone decided whether to laugh or not. Then Lala Lamb piped up in her clear, high voice.

"And sailing ships," she said. "There used to be lots of big sailing ships – you know, with sails – to use up the wind, as well."

Biggy Pig felt that the conversation was getting out of hand (or out of trotter, I should say). "Never mind *why* there's more wind," he said, "we've got to find a better way of dealing with it."

Just then one of Farmer Barnes' sheets, which he had put on the line to dry in the wind, flapped past. It had escaped!

Without thinking for a moment what he was doing, Biggy Pig grabbed the passing sheet with two trotters – and took off! The world's first hang-gliding pig sailed over the farmyard, having the time of his life.

"And they say pigs may fly!" Dymphna sniffed. But Duchess was all eagerness. "At least he's using up the wind!" she cried. "Come on everyone! There are lots more sheets on the line!"

Busy Hen covered her eyes with her wings. Someone was sure to get hurt. But whether Biggy Pig was using up the wind, or whether it just dropped of its own accord, the day was suddenly very still.

All the animals were disappointed, except Biggy Pig, who had had a wonderful time, even if he hadn't planned on a water landing!

Mrs Marchant's Visit

Farmer Barnes didn't have many visitors. It wasn't because he was an unfriendly man. It was simply that he hardly ever had time to do anything other than work on the farm. So when he started tidying up the yard one day, the animals got very excited.

"Someone's coming, mark my words," said Busy Hen. "The last time he did this was when his sister from Australia came."

"Maybe he's found a wife," said Dymphna, hopefully.

"But he hasn't met anyone," replied Busy Hen impatiently. She always found Dymphna annoying.

"Well, I don't know how it is with humans. He might have been able to ring up and order one," protested Dymphna. "Like he does the chicken feed, you know."

Busy Hen stalked off in disgust. Dymphna really had no grasp of the real world. "Too much time in the water," muttered the hen. "Her brain's gone soggy."

The animals didn't have long to wait for the visitor. Two days later, a shiny car swept into the yard. A lady got out and walked delicately across to the farmhouse on her high heels, watching all the time to see if she was stepping in anything messy.

Before the lady even reached the farmhouse, Farmer Barnes came out. He was wearing his old suit.

"Mr Barnes, how do you do?" said the lady. "Will you show me around?"

"Mrs Marchant? Please come right this way," replied the farmer.

"He likes her," squealed Dymphna, jumping up and down. "She's going to be Mrs Barnes!"

"Be quiet, Dymphna!" whispered Busy Hen. "She's here for *business*. Anyone can see that."

Dymphna wasn't sure what business was, so she crept around the pond to a place where she could watch through the weeds.

"I think we can agree your loan," said Mrs Marchant, as she climbed back into her car.

Dymphna trotted back and reported to the other animals. "She's not going to marry him," she said sadly. "She said, 'I think we can agree you're alone.'"

Busy Hen sighed. She would have to explain to the other animals later that Farmer Barnes' loan for the new barn was his only business with Mrs Marchant.

Little Pig Gets Lost

Although there were lots of piglets on Windytop Farm, one in particular caught Farmer Barnes' eye. Like his great uncle, Biggy Pig, he had all the signs of being a champion, and Farmer Barnes did like to win ribbons at the County Show. He called the piglet Little Pig. Of course, like Biggy, Little Pig had a long, grand name as well, but no one could ever remember what it was.

Farmer Barnes wanted Little Pig to grow big and fat, like you-know-who, but Little Pig surprised everyone by wanting to do sports! He liked to go for a run every morning and to find lots of time for jumping and diving practice.

"He'll never put weight on at this rate," said Biggy Pig, shaking his head.

Then, one day, Little Pig went missing. At first everyone thought he had gone for a longer run than usual, but when he didn't come back by lunchtime, and his feed trough was still full, all the animals began to get worried.

"He is only a little pig," said Duchess the cow. "He's not old enough to look after himself in the big, wide world."

"We need to search the farm," said Biggy. "The sheep can look in the meadows. I'll check the barns. The hens and ducks can look along the hedges and bushes. And you, Duchess, can wait here in case Little Pig comes home. I do hope he hasn't come to any harm."

But an hour later, the animals returned to the yard without Little Pig. They were now very worried indeed. They sat together, trying to think of a new plan. It was just then that Biggy's sharp ears heard a little squealing sound.

Hardly able to believe their eyes, the animals looked up, and up, and up … right to the top of the tree. A little pink face looked down at them. "I was climbing," said Little Pig, "but I got stuck!"

Busy Hen and Dymphna soon fluttered about and guided Little Pig down. He was very grateful.

You know, after that, Little Pig wasn't quite so keen to test his sporting abilities.

"If you keep snuffling in your feed trough like that," said Busy Hen, "you'll soon be even bigger than Biggy Pig!"

And he was!

Cackle Crows Again

One morning, the sun was already high in the sky when Farmer Barnes came stomping out of the farmhouse.

"I don't know what's the matter with me," he muttered. "I don't think I've ever woken up late before. Poor old Duchess will be wondering where I am."

The first thing Farmer Barnes did every morning was to milk Duchess the cow. He expected to see her waiting at the gate, anxiously looking out for him. He was amazed to see that Duchess was fast asleep under a tree, with Delilah snuggled next to her.

It was the same when Farmer Barnes finished the milking and went to feed Biggy Pig. Biggy was a pig who liked his breakfast – and his lunch, and his supper, and several little snacks in between – so the farmer was surprised to find Biggy snoring in a corner instead of tapping his trotters impatiently on his sty.

Farmer Barnes hurried off to check on the other animals. All of them were sleeping peacefully. The puzzled farmer was just about to telephone the vet to tell him that there was a bad case of sleeping sickness on the farm, when it struck him that all the animals seemed quite well as soon as they were awakened. Then, all of a sudden, he realized what the problem was. Every creature on the farm, including Farmer Barnes, was awakened each morning by Cackle the rooster, crowing at the top of his voice. This morning, Cackle simply hadn't crowed!

When Farmer Barnes finally found Cackle hiding in a corner of the barn, he couldn't help laughing. As usual, Cackle had been poking his beak into places he shouldn't. Farmer Barnes had left a bucket of tar, which he had been using to mend the barn roof, behind the farmhouse. Before it had cooled and dried, Cackle had let his curiosity get the better of him. Now he couldn't open his beak to cackle, crow or peck at his breakfast.

So Farmer Barnes called the vet after all. He was soon able to clean up the silly bird and give him a good talking-to about how important it was to brush his beak after every meal.

And for a whole week after that, neither Farmer Barnes nor the rest of the animals grumbled and groaned when Cackle began to crow at the crack of dawn. They didn't even complain when he gave them extra-early double crowing to celebrate being able to open his beak!

Mrs Speckles and the Cat

When Mrs Speckles is upset about something, *everyone* knows it. That hen can make even more noise and fuss than Cackle. *Cluck! Cluck! CLUCK!* She flutters and flaps her way around the farm, making sure no one is in any doubt about what is bothering her.

One morning, Mrs Speckles was more upset than usual.

"It's that cat!" she cried. "She's sitting on the henhouse roof and she's been there all night! It's not as if she really lives here!"

It was true. The fat, fluffy cat who spent all her time on the farm really belonged to an old lady down the road. Each morning, the old lady brushed Pompom, as she called her cat, and tied a beautiful bow around her neck. Then Pompom proudly walked down the path from the front door and wasn't seen again until suppertime! The old lady had no idea that her cat spent every day on Windytop Farm.

When the other animals heard what Mrs Speckles was saying, even they were a little concerned. Pompom never spent the night on the farm. She had a cosy bed at home. And her beautiful bow was definitely looking bedraggled this morning.

"There's no doubt about it," hissed Busy Hen to her friend. "She hasn't been home since yesterday."

Just then, Farmer Barnes came out of the farmhouse. He walked through the yard, looking to left and right. When he spotted Pompom he came right over and picked her up.

"I thought you might be here," he said. "Your mistress had to move to a special home, where she can be looked after properly. She can't take you with her, so she has asked me if I will look after you. Of course, I will. But there is one thing. I'm not much use at tying bows, you know, not with these big old fingers. You're a farm cat now. So this will have to go." And he gently pulled Pompom's bow from around her neck.

Of course, the other animals were listening. "What use is she going to be?" hissed Mrs Speckles. "She's just another mouth to feed."

But just then, one of the little mice who lived in the old henhouse took advantage of the commotion to have a little look around in the new henhouse. The hens spotted him with horror. But so did someone else. In a flash, Pompom dashed into the henhouse and chased the mouse out.

Mrs Speckles looked at Busy Hen. Busy Hen nodded wisely.

As Pompom strolled back, Mrs Speckles went boldly forward. "Welcome to Windytop Farm," she said. "We're all very glad you'll be staying with us from now on."

The Trouble With Denby Dog

Farmer Barnes took good care of all his animals, but Denby Dog was special. He had worked with the farmer for more years than either of them could remember, in sunshine and rain, when the wind was howling around Windytop Farm and when the snow was deep on the ground. Farmer Barnes couldn't imagine life without Denby.

But Denby Dog was getting old. He found it harder to run after the tractor as Farmer Barnes drove out of the yard. His legs felt stiff as he trotted up the lane. Even his bark was not as loud as it used to be.

As winter approached, Farmer Barnes became more and more worried about Denby.

"Old fellow," he said, "the wind is bitter this morning. Why not stay beside the fire or in your kennel in the yard? I can manage without you today."

But the old dog gave Farmer Barnes such a mournful look that he couldn't bear to leave him behind. Later, Denby Dog explained to his friend Biggy Pig how he felt.

"I've been with Farmer Barnes for years, pup and dog," he said. "What if something happened to him away in the fields and I wasn't there to run for help? I'd never forgive myself. No, while there's life in these old bones, I must do my job."

Strangely enough, it was also to Biggy Pig that Farmer Barnes explained his worries that evening. He leaned over the sty wall and scratched Biggy's back.

"It's like this," he said. "Old Denby simply isn't up to the job any more. I've bought a new pup. He'll be arriving tomorrow, but I hate the idea of hurting the old boy's feelings."

Biggy Pig snorted in a comforting sort of way. He felt sure everything would be fine. And it was.

When the new puppy arrived, Denby Dog got straight down to business. "It's high time I retired, young pup," he said. "And now that there'll be someone to follow in my pawprints, I can do it at last. But first, there's a lot I've got to teach you. Follow me now, and leave those chickens alone!"

These days, Denby Dog has a leisurely life, chatting with his friends and lying in the sun. After all, he deserves it.

Dymphna to the Rescue

Dymphna Duck and Busy Hen were never best friends, but one day something happened that made Busy Hen almost fond of Dymphna. It was during a very busy time on the farm, when Farmer Barnes was hard at work in the fields from morning until night. At such times, he asked his old friend Annie to come each day to take care of the animals.

Now Annie was not the most efficient person. She was likely to forget things and drop things and take twice as long to do a simple job as most people – especially if Farmer Barnes was watching. Busy Hen liked Annie and sympathized. She herself found it very hard to lay an egg if someone was watching her. Besides, Annie was very fond of the animals, and anyone can forgive a knocked-over grain bucket or a late lunch for that.

One morning Farmer Barnes left Annie in charge. "The mechanic is coming to have a look at my old tractor this morning," he said, as he set off to the fields on his new tractor. "Here are the keys. They're the only set I've got, so please don't lose them."

Annie put the keys in her pocket. Then, as Farmer Barnes rumbled away, she set off to fetch Biggy Pig's breakfast. But on the way – and this was typical of Annie – she was sidetracked by the sight of a little duckling sitting forlornly in a puddle in the middle of the yard.

"Poor little thing," said Annie, picking up the duckling. "Can't you find your way back to the pond? Here!" She carefully leaned out into the pond and gently put the duckling onto the water. As she did so, there was a loud splash. The tractor keys had fallen out of her pocket and into the water!

"Oh!" cried Annie. "Oh no!" She hurried off to find the yard broom, to see if she could feel the keys at the bottom of the pond and fish them out. But the bottom of the pond was very muddy. It seemed hopeless.

Busy Hen – as usual – had seen everything that happened. She at once hurried off to find Biggy Pig.

"You like wallowing about in mud, Biggy," she cried. "Can't you find those keys for Annie?"

"My diving days are over," sighed Biggy. "Mud is one thing, but water is quite another."

Busy Hen had run out of ideas, and Annie was close to tears, when Dymphna Duck strolled up with something jangling from her beak. "Is this what you're looking for?" she asked, dropping the keys at Annie's feet.

Annie was so grateful to Dymphna that she gave her the ham and mustard sandwiches from her lunchbox. And it just shows what a nice duck Dymphna is that she shared them all with Busy Hen – although the fact that Annie is as clumsy with mustard as she is with keys might have had something to do with it too!

Farmer Barnes' Spring Clean

Farmer Barnes is a man who never gives two minutes' thought to the brand of washing powder he uses or whether his kitchen is painted a fashionable shade. As long as something works, he doesn't mind too much what it looks like, which is obvious from his clothes.

But he does like things to be clean, and on a busy farm that's pretty difficult. So that is why, once a year, Farmer Barnes has his big Spring Clean. *Everything* gets cleaned, from the cupboard under the sink to the roof of Biggy Pig's sty.

You've never seen so much washing and brushing, dusting and polishing. All the animals join in. Biggy Pig is good at snuffling dust out of corners, while Busy Hen's beady eyes can spot the tiniest speck of dirt at twenty paces. Dymphna Duck and her friends love anything to do with water, so they splash about in buckets of bubbles all day long. One year, they started to try to shampoo the sheep and had to be stopped by Farmer Barnes.

The last stage of the Spring Clean takes place in the farmhouse. Farmer Barnes carries all the furniture out into the yard and vacuums the house from top to bottom. Then he carries the tables and chairs and beds back into the house and plonks himself down on the sofa. Spring Cleaning is over for another year.

But this year, as Farmer Barnes vacuumed furiously, his old vacuum cleaner making the most extraordinary noises, something dreadful happened. It started to rain! Not just a little gentle shower, but pouring down, splashing on the table and making puddles on the chairs.

"He'll be cross," said Busy Hen anxiously, sheltering under a stool.

"He'll shout and stomp about," agreed Mrs Speckles. "I don't want to be around when *that* starts."

Then, as suddenly as it began, the rain stopped.

A few minutes later, Farmer Barnes appeared in the yard. He looked at the soggy furniture. His face went red. His forehead furrowed. The animals waited for the second storm of the day.

Then the farmer began to laugh. "This is the cleanest my furniture has *ever* been," he roared. "Let's hope this happens every year!"

Lala Lamb's Singing Soirée

One morning after breakfast, when the animals were wandering off to do whatever they had planned for the day, they were surprised to hear someone banging a stick on the rain barrel.

"Excuse me!" called a little voice. "Attention, please! Listen!"

It was little Lala Lamb, standing as bold as anything in the middle of the yard. As soon as she was sure all the animals were listening, Lala began her Important Announcement.

"This evening," she said, "I am holding a soirée in the small barn. There will be singing (from me) and all other animals are asked to perform."

Harold the horse asked what everyone else was wondering. "What's a swaray?" he asked. "Will we all have to hold it?"

"No, no," laughed Lala. "A soirée is a kind of musical party. Daphne Duck told me the word. She learnt it from that French Hen she knew. Now, I want everyone to be ready at seven o'clock."

By the end of the day, Farmer Barnes was very worried about his animals. He had come across Biggy Pig making the most extraordinary noise behind the pig sty. He didn't know that Biggy was getting ready for the evening.

Later, Farmer Barnes found Busy Hen and half a dozen other hens skipping about in a very strange way. He wondered if a bee was buzzing among them. He didn't know they were preparing for their ballet performance.

As for Harold the horse, Farmer Barnes could hardly believe his ears when he heard Harold mooing and clucking over the stable door. He didn't know that Harold was doing his impressions.

That evening, when Farmer Barnes went in for his supper, everyone gathered in the small barn and the soirée began. It was wonderful! The animals couldn't remember when they had enjoyed themselves so much, even if everyone did think that Biggy's song was an impression of an elephant, and the hens' ballet kicked up so much dust that it was hard to see their footwork.

As a Grand Finale, all the animals sang the Official Farm Song.

Oh, Farmer Barnes he had a farm,
Ee-i-ee-i-o!
And on that farm lived Biggy Pig,
Ee-i-ee-i-o!
With a grunt, snort here,
And a grunt, snort there,
Here a grunt, there a snort,
Everywhere a grunt, snort!
Farmer Barnes he had a farm,
Ee-i-ee-i-o!

Can you sing the rest of the verses?

Where's Duchess's Hat?

After a few blustery days, Farmer Barnes found he had a lot of repairs to attend to on Windytop Farm. There were tiles missing from the farmhouse roof, large branches to be cleared from the lanes, and one or two fences had fallen down. With so much to think about, it's not surprising that Farmer Barnes wasn't concentrating by the time he was doing his last repair job of the day … putting Scary Scarecrow upright again in the top field. Scary was called Scary because he really wasn't! He was the friendliest-looking scarecrow you've ever seen, and birds from miles around used to come and perch on his hat and shoulders for a chat. Farmer Barnes knew this, but he figured that while birds were chatting, they weren't pecking at his seeds, so that was okay.

Farmer Barnes set Scary Scarecrow firmly upright in the field again and was just about to walk away, when he noticed that Scary no longer had his hat. The farmer looked around. It must have been blown in the wind, but surely it couldn't be far away. Aha! Farmer Barnes spotted a straw hat under the hedge and hurried to scoop it up and plonk it on Scary's head. It looked fine.

But back in the farmyard, someone else was missing a hat! Duchess the cow had lost hers in the wind as well. She sent Delilah the calf and Lala Lamb off to look for it.

Now neither Delilah nor Lala could quite remember what Duchess's hat looked like. They were small animals, and the hat was usually high up on Duchess's head, so it was only when Duchess was lying down that they had a good view. And neither of those young animals was very good at remembering things.

That is why, when Lala and Delilah found a handsome top hat lying under a gate, they brought it straight back to Duchess, full of pride that they had succeeded.

Seeing their eager little faces, Duchess hadn't the heart to be cross. She rather liked her jaunty new headgear, but all the other animals laughed until their sides ached. Lala and Delilah couldn't understand why.

"My dears," smiled Duchess, "you just come with me. We're going to visit a certain scarecrow. He's got something I need, and I believe I have something of his. Fair exchange is no robbery, as they say."

As she passed the duck pond, Duchess had one last look at herself. "Maybe it's not really *me*," she said, "but you'd think the others would realize that a stylish cow like me can carry anything off!"

The Pie Contest

Farmer Barnes always worked hard, but sometimes he worked too hard. One autumn day, he tried to lift a bag of grain that was simply too heavy – and dropped it on his foot. The hens watched anxiously as he gave a yell and hobbled slowly into the house to call the doctor.

"I don't want you to put any weight on that foot for a week," said the doctor firmly, when she arrived. "Stay in your chair, catch up on some reading, and let your friends take the strain for a while. It's high time you had a rest."

Farmer Barnes grumbled and groaned, but he knew the doctor was right. Anyway, his foot was far too painful to walk on. Farmer Barnes was just beginning to wonder how he would manage as far as food was concerned, when his visitors started to arrive, one by one.

First Mrs Mannheim from the next farm rushed into the living room.

"I knew you wouldn't be able to get up, so I let myself in," she cried. "And I've brought you one of my extra special chocolate-marshmallow-delight pies. That will keep your spirits up!"

Half an hour later, Miss Florence Fong, from the grocery in town, crept in and peeped around the door.

"I heard about your accident," she said, "and I've made you my lemon-orange-and-pineapple pie, with caramel cream. Everyone seems to like it."

Later that day, Mr Baxter from the bakery came around with a maple-and-walnut-banana-and-meringue pie. Mrs Marvel from the local restaurant brought a *tarte aux cerises avec mousse au chocolat blanc* (whatever *that* was), and the doctor herself dropped by with a wholemeal-muesli-oatmeal-and-date pie.

"Sorry!" she laughed. "It's a bit solid. I'm not very good at cooking. But it will do you good!"

That evening, Annie came in from the yard.

"I couldn't get here before," she said, "because there was a lot to do on the farm, but I have made you a pie to keep you going."

Farmer Barnes eyed the ordinary-looking pie.

"What's in it?" he asked.

"I'm afraid it's just a plain apple pie," said Annie. "Oh dear, I can see you've already got lots of beautiful fancy pies."

"And they're *all* too rich and sticky for me," said Farmer Barnes. "A plain apple pie is just what I feel like. I can always rely on you, Annie."

So Farmer Barnes enjoyed his apple pie and felt much better afterwards. As for the other pies, they were very much enjoyed as well … by Biggy Pig, Harold Horse, Lala Lamb, Duchess, Delilah, Mrs Speckles, Busy Hen, Cackle, Dymphna … in fact, all the animals on Windytop Farm!

Farmer Barnes Goes to Town

While Farmer Barnes was resting his injured foot, Annie looked after the farm, and she did it very well. If there was anyone who cared as much about the animals as the farmer himself, it was Annie.

"You know," Duchess the cow confessed to Busy Hen, "I wouldn't mind if Farmer Barnes took a little longer to recover. Annie talks to me so nicely during milking."

"I know what you mean," clucked Busy Hen.

One morning, when Annie was feeding the ducks, there came a grumbling and a shouting from Farmer Barnes' open bedroom window.

"Oh, I wonder what the matter is," cried Annie, hoping the farmer hadn't dropped something *else* on his foot.

Dymphna Duck quacked loudly. She knew exactly what was going on. It didn't happen very often, but when Farmer Barnes went to town, he liked to look a bit smarter than usual. And the grumbling and shouting were because he always got cross with the fiddly little buttons on his best shirt. Somehow his big, strong hands weren't made for such things.

At last Farmer Barnes was ready and set off for town.

"Didn't he look smart?" Annie said to Mrs Speckles. "I expect he was going to the bank."

Mrs Speckles fluttered off to talk to her friend Busy Hen. She believed Farmer Barnes needed a wife, and she felt Mrs Marchant at the bank was very suitable.

But Busy Hen clucked impatiently. "Mrs Marchant would be quite out of place on a farm," she said. "Farmer Barnes needs someone like … someone like …" and Busy Hen suddenly looked very thoughtful indeed.

When Farmer Barnes arrived home later that day, he was carrying a big box and looking anxious. He marched straight over to where Annie was clearing out Harold's stable and pushed the box toward her.

"Just wanted to say thank you," he said gruffly, "for all your hard work, you know. Don't know what we'd have done without you."

Annie went pink and peeped into the box. For a few seconds she was speechless. Then she pulled out the prettiest hat you've ever seen.

"I don't know about these things," said Farmer Barnes, looking uncomfortable. "But the lady in the shop said you'd like it."

As Annie at last found her voice. Mrs Speckles tut-tutted.

"Not at all the right present for Annie," she muttered, remembering Busy Hen's words. "Quite out of place on a farm."

But Busy Hen was doing a little dance of joy all by herself.

"No," she said, "it was *just* right. It was absolutely *perfect*."

A Name for a Newcomer

Each year, lots of babies were born on Windytop Farm. Farmer Barnes liked to give names to them all, and he was pretty good at remembering them, too.

But one year, there were so many babies, he had to struggle to think of new names for all of them. There were twenty-four baby ducklings. There were seventeen baby chicks. Add to that nineteen baby lambs, seven little goslings, and Duchess's new calf, and you have a lot of babies.

To make things simpler, Farmer Barnes worked out his own system. He decided to give the chicks names beginning with C, like Charlie and Caroline and Chuckles and Cobweb. The lambs had names beginning with L, like Lucy and Lawrie and Lavender and Lightfoot. The goslings, of course, had names like Gordon and Gerda and George.

It was when he came to the ducklings that Farmer Barnes had problems. He simply could not think of twenty-four names beginning with D, especially as several other animals on the farm, such as Duchess and Delilah, already had D-names.

By the end of the week, after a lot of thought and asking the advice of anyone who came to the farm, Farmer Barnes had twenty-three names, but he was well and truly stuck on the last one. No matter how hard he thought, he simply couldn't come up with another name.

It so happened that the next day, Farmer Barnes' niece paid him a surprise visit, bringing along her baby daughter. All children seemed to like Farmer Barnes. He soon had the little one in fits of giggles. Then he took her and her mother on a tour of the farm.

The baby loved seeing the animals. Last of all, Farmer Barnes took her to the duck pond.

"Here," he said, "is my biggest problem. What would be a good name for a duck, Rosie-Mae?"

Rosie-Mae didn't hesitate. "Duck!" she cried. "Duck! Duck!"

Farmer Barnes laughed out loud. Then he stopped laughing.

"You know," he said, "that's not such a bad idea!"

And that is why, to this day, after he has called Dolores and Deirdre and Darcy and Della and all their brothers and sisters, Farmer Barnes yells "Duck-duck!" and the last little duckling (who's not so little now) comes scuttling along.

Ready, Set, Go!

With so many baby animals on Windytop Farm, the older animals were busy night and day keeping an eye on them. Even Biggy Pig became accustomed to sleeping with one eye open, in case *another* little duckling dived over the edge of his sty and got stuck in the mud.

As the babies grew older, things got even worse. Although they were much more independent now, they were also much more likely to wander off into the fields – but still not able to find their way home again. Evening after evening, Harold clip-clopped up the lane, calling to all the chicks and ducklings and goslings who had strayed from the farmyard.

One evening, when all the little ones had been rounded up at last, Busy Hen called them together for a Serious Talk. She didn't mince her words. She told them about fast cars, foxes, hawks, and hunters, until they all looked suitably anxious.

"In future," said Busy Hen, "when you want to go somewhere, you must all go together. There's safety in numbers."

After that, it was a common sight to see a long line of baby animals winding its way down the lane and across the fields.

For a while, everything was fine. Then, one evening, the little ones didn't come home! Biggy Pig and Busy Hen set off to find them. They soon came across the little ones far away in the Top Field.

"It's too far to walk home," explained one little duckling. "We're tired. Our little legs won't walk that far. They might even drop off!"

"That's right!" cheeped the others. "We're only small, you know."

"Oh, so you won't be able to take place in the Special Sunset Race, then?" sighed Busy Hen.

"It's a shame," said Biggy Pig.

"What race?" squeaked the little ones. "We're ready! We're ready!"

"The winner is the first one back to the farmyard," said Busy Hen. "Ready? Set! Go!"

Those naughty babies ran off as fast as their little legs would carry them. Busy Hen and Biggy Pig followed them at a more leisurely pace.

"Who won?" asked Biggy, when they reached the yard.

"It was a photo finish!" Harold smiled. "Only we didn't have a photo. We're just going to have to hold the Special Sunset race *every* night until we're sure."

The babies would have cheered, but they were all asleep – every one.

Biggy Pig's Dancing Lesson

Busy Hen was very busy these days. She was giving all the new chicks and ducklings dancing lessons – and one or two older birds were joining in as well.

"Is it some new fitness craze, Busy?" asked Harold the horse, seeing several ducks bowing their heads this way and that while trying to balance on one foot.

"It's just dancing, Harold," replied Busy Hen. "Further to the left, Dymphna! Don't let that wing droop!"

"But why, Busy Hen? I mean, why is everyone so keen on dancing *now*?"

The dancing teacher looked mysterious. "You never know," she said, "when there might be some kind of … well … party or something."

Before long, it was clear to all the animals that the ducks and chicks were becoming very good at their dancing. In fact, lessons drew quite a crowd as Busy Hen put her pupils through their paces.

One morning, just as her class had finished, Busy Hen heard a strange sound coming from the pig sty.

"*Pssssst! Psssst!*"

It was Biggy Pig, trying to attract her attention.

"What's the matter, Biggy?" asked Busy Hen. "Have you lost your voice?"

"No!" whispered the pig. "I just didn't want the other animals to hear. I wanted to talk to you about having dancing lessons."

Busy Hen was surprised, but she tried not to show it.

"Of course, Biggy," she said. "You're welcome to join us any morning."

"I'd be too embarrassed," replied Biggy. "Could I have a private lesson? Say, tonight after dark?"

That night, some extraordinary sounds were heard coming from Biggy's sty. *Bang!* Something hard (like a trotter) hit a feed trough. *Thwack!* Something large (like a bottom) hit a wall. *Ouch!* Something squishy (like a snuffly nose) got too near a flailing foot.

"It's no good, Biggy," said Busy Hen in the darkness. "You can't learn in here. It's too small. Come out into the meadow."

And that is why the smallest chick, opening one sleepy eye at midnight, saw a wonderful sight. It was a pig, dancing in front of the huge harvest moon, and dancing *beautifully.*

A Wife for Farmer Barnes

These days, Annie seemed to be helping out more and more on the farm. Even when Farmer Barnes' foot was better, he still seemed to need her. The animals were pleased because they liked Annie, and Busy Hen kept her beady eyes open all the time. She didn't want to miss anything exciting. She was certain that Annie and Farmer Barnes should get married, and she felt that it was just a matter of time before the farmer popped the question.

But days passed. Weeks passed. Months passed. The weather grew colder. Annie tramped into the yard early each morning, her breath making clouds in the frosty air.

"If she lived here, she wouldn't have that cold journey down the lane," Busy Hen told Cackle, seeing Annie rubbing her poor red hands together. "I don't know what's the matter with the man," muttered Busy Hen. "He can't see a good thing when it's right in front of his nose."

"Well, it's tricky for a chap," said Cackle. "He's probably afraid she'd say no, and then things on the farm would be difficult. I can understand it. You can't go rushing into these things."

"Well, you would say that, wouldn't you?" retorted Busy Hen. "You never did get up the courage to ask *me* to marry *you*. In the end, I had to do it."

"I can't see Annie saying anything to Farmer Barnes, though," said Cackle. "She's much too ladylike. *Ouch!* Mind what you're doing with your beak, Busy Hen!"

On this occasion, Cackle, as so many times in the past, was completely wrong. One day, Annie marched into the yard carrying a Christmas tree under one arm and a box of trimmings under the other.

"What's that?" asked Farmer Barnes.

"It will be Christmas soon," said Annie, "and I can't bear the thought of you being all by yourself. Christmas is a time for families."

"But…" began Farmer Barnes.

"But you're all on your own, I know," said Annie. "And so am I. I've waited long enough for you to say something, Fred, but I can see I'm just going to have to do it myself. It's high time you got married."

"But…" said Farmer Barnes, looking pink and happy at the same time.

"Yes, I mean me," laughed Annie, but she suddenly wasn't able to say another word.

"Disgraceful!" squawked Mrs Speckles. "Kissing in the farmyard! Whatever next?"

But Busy Hen was hugging Cackle with delight. "I think it's lovely," she said.

127

Tree Trouble

When it is windy on Windytop Farm, as you know, it is *very* windy. One night, the animals covered their ears as they snuggled down in their straw, for a gale was blowing. At first they heard only the howling of the wind. Later there was clattering and clanging as tiles flew from the farmhouse roof and feed troughs tumbled across the farmyard.

The animals didn't feel worried. They were all safe and warm in their stables, or sties, or henhouses, or barns. Busy Hen had helped count the little chicks to make sure they were safe inside – and that took a very long time as they kept scuttling about and hiding in the straw. In the barn, Dymphna was having the same trouble with the ducklings. Poor Dymphna! As well as the noise outside, the ducklings were having a contest to make howling-wind noises!

128

It wasn't until the next day that the full extent of the storm damage was obvious. A great tree had fallen across the farmyard, only just missing the henhouse and barricading Harold in his stable. Of course, this wasn't the first time that a tree had been blown down on Windytop Farm, but this one had done dreadful damage as it fell.

Farmer Barnes was almost in tears as he looked at the scene in the farmyard. All he could think about was the time it would take and the money it would cost to put everything right again.

Just then Annie arrived and looked around.

"Well," she said, "that *was* lucky!"

"Lucky?" said Farmer Barnes faintly. "How can you call this lucky?"

Annie was smiling. "Not a single animal was hurt," she said, "and neither were you, Fred. I call that very lucky indeed."

Farmer Barnes grinned. "You're right," he said, "as always. Don't worry, Harold, we'll have you free in no time. After all, it's Christmas in a couple of days and we need to be straight by then, don't we?"

Buzz! Buzz!

Christmas had come at last to Windytop Farm and all the animals were enjoying it enormously. In the morning, Annie put a special treat in each pail of breakfast feed. Harold had some juicy apples. The hens had a special corn and seed mixture. Biggy Pig even had some of Farmer Barnes' own plum pudding!

There were presents, too. Duchess was given a new hat (it was one of Annie's old ones, but it looked very fine trimmed with some new ribbon). Harold became the proud owner of a sign with his name on it above the stable door. There was something for everyone, and the whole farmyard was filled with the sound of happy, chuckling birds and animals.

Only Biggy Pig wasn't feeling on top of the world. At first he thought maybe the plum pudding was disagreeing with him. But after thinking hard about his tummy for a few minutes, he decided that all was well in that department! No, the problem was something else. Gradually, the pig realized what was annoying him. There was a strange buzzing sound very near his left ear.

Buzz! Buzz! Buzz! Buzz!

Biggy described the problem to Busy Hen. "It's obvious, Biggy," she replied. "It's a bee!"

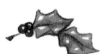

Biggy Pig felt relieved for maybe two minutes. Then common sense told him bees simply are not around during the winter. They are snuggled up in their hives somewhere. They are not buzzing around annoying innocent pigs. But if it wasn't a bee, what was it?

Harold the horse, who had clopped by to wish Biggy a Merry Christmas, had another suggestion.

"Buzzing," he said wisely, "is very often caused by something electrical. There are a lot of buzzing things in Farmer Barnes' kitchen. Some of them beep, too. Are you sure it isn't a beeping and not a buzzing you can hear? (Harold himself was a little hard of hearing these days, but then he was a very elderly horse.)

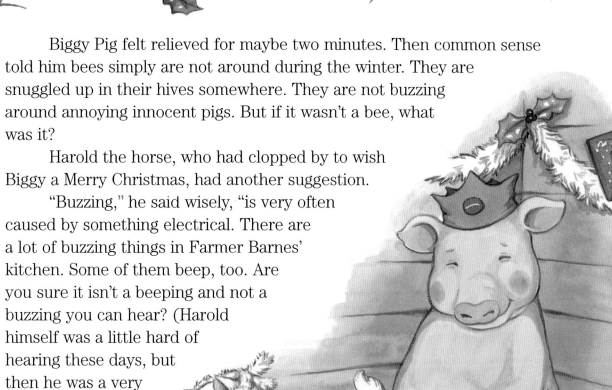

Biggy Pig knew perfectly well whether he was hearing a beeping or a buzzing. Only the holiday season stopped him from telling Harold so rather sharply. Then, just as Biggy felt he couldn't stand the buzzing any longer, along came Pompom the cat.

"So *you've* got it, Biggy!" she cried. "I didn't think pigs were interested in such things."

She pounced into a corner of Biggy's sty and came out with … a clockwork mouse! It had run in under the gate and got stuck!

"Thank you, Pig!" purred Pompom. "And Merry Christmas!"

"And to you, Pompom," replied Biggy. "And a very *peaceful* New Year to all of us," he smiled, looking meaningfully at the mouse.

"*Buzz! Buzz!*" said the mouse. And what *that* meant is anybody's guess!

The Moon Pig

Biggy Pig was waiting patiently for his breakfast one morning when he noticed the sun was already peeping over the barn roof. Biggy's tummy felt odd. It knew perfectly well that when the sun was as high as *that* in the sky, it was well past breakfast time. Where was Annie? It was very strange.

A few minutes later, he heard the clanking of buckets, and Farmer Barnes looked over the door of the sty.

"Here's your breakfast, old friend," he said. "Sorry it's a bit late, but I don't want Annie overdoing things."

Biggy might have thought that was strange too, but he already had his head deep in the feed trough and he didn't hear a word.

Little Pig was not so greedy. He heard everything Farmer Barnes said, and later, when Biggy was resting his (very full) tummy, he began to wonder out loud about what was happening on Windytop Farm.

"It's very mysterious," said Little Pig, "and my dear Philomena agrees with me. There have been several strange happenings recently. Lots of the animals have noticed it."

"Like what?" yawned Biggy, thinking it was time for his morning nap.

"Like the eggs not being collected on time," said Little Pig. "Like Annie not coming to scratch my back like she used to do. Like the farmyard being so untidy. Like Annie wearing Farmer Barnes' clothes – I think that's very odd."

"I think she's got too fat for her clothes," said Biggy Pig, who knew a thing or too about getting fat and thought it was the best thing that could happen to anyone – or any pig.

"I still think it's strange," said Little Pig. "But there are odd things that are really spooky, too. Like the Moon Pig."

"The Moon Pig?" asked Harold the horse, who had been shamelessly eavesdropping during the pigs' conversation.

"Yes," said Little Pig, pleased to have a bigger audience. "When the Moon Pig turns blue, that means strange and wonderful things are going to happen. And the Moon Pig has been blue all this week."

"It's just the time of year," said Harold. "The moon always looks blue around now. And anyway, I don't know what you mean about the Moon Pig. It's obviously a horse in the moon. Everyone knows that."

But that night, Little Pig gazed up at the moon and whispered to himself. "I don't care what Harold says. Something strange and wonderful *is* going to happen. And it's going to happen soon."

Five-Minute
Kitten
Tales

Meet the Little Kittens!

When a mother cat has *five* little kittens to take care of, she certainly has her paws full!

Honeybun

Rolypoly

Tiger Tail

Fluffy

Mopsy

Contents

Where's That Kitten?

When a mother cat has *five* little kittens to take care of, she certainly has her paws full! She just can't keep her eyes on all of them at once.

One morning, Mamma Cat was busy giving her babies their breakfast. "One bowl of porridge for you, and one for you, and one for you, and one for you, and one... Just a minute, where's that kitten?" The fifth little kitten was nowhere to be seen.

Mamma Cat looked under the beds and in the closets. She checked in the laundry basket and hunted through the toy box. But there was no little kitten to be found.

"Now then," said Mamma Cat, "one of you kittens must know where your brother is. Well, Fluffy?"

"I don't know," mewed Fluffy.

"What about you, Rolypoly?"

"I haven't seen him at all."

"And have you seen your brother, Mopsy," asked her mother, "with your bright little eyes?"

"No, Mamma," said Mopsy.

But when Mamma Cat turned to Honeybun, it was as plain as could be that the kitten knew *something*.

"Well?" asked Mamma Cat.

"He's gone on an adventure," explained Honeybun.

"An adventure? What sort of an adventure?"

"He's … well … it's a *climbing* adventure…."

Mamma Cat frowned and sighed. "A climbing adventure indeed! I hope he took an oxygen mask."

"W-what?" stammered Honeybun.

"In very high places, the air is really thin," explained Mamma Cat. "It would be difficult for a little kitten to breathe without extra oxygen. And that could be very, very dangerous."

Before Honeybun could say another word, they all heard a plaintive little sound.

"Help!" called someone from a very high place. "Help! Meow! Help!"

Mamma Cat didn't need to look around. She reached straight up to the top of the closet and scooped up one frightened little kitten.

"Well, Tiger Tail," she said, "your climbing is certainly very good. But didn't you *want* any breakfast?"

"Oh," said poor Tiger Tail, "my climbing *up* is very good, but my climbing *down* needs more practice. And, of course, without oxygen…"

"I have heard," said Mamma Cat with a smile, "that porridge is just as good as oxygen in some situations. No more climbing, please, until *after* breakfast!"

Tiger Tail Trouble

Some little kittens, like some little children, just can't help getting into trouble. They try as hard as they can to be good. They don't mean to throw pudding over visiting cats – but still Great Aunt Flora has to wash her whiskers. They do take care of their clothes – but still one glove, one sock, and a woolly hat with a pompom on top get stuck at the top of a tree. They run as fast as they can to get home in time for supper, but still Mamma Cat is waiting grimly on the doorstep with a plate of burnt sausages.

     Tiger Tail was a kitten just like that. His father had taken him aside for a Serious Talk more than once, but still Tiger Tail got into trouble almost every day.

     One morning, Tiger Tail looked at the calendar and saw that it was Mother's Day. Fluffy, Rolypoly, Mopsy, and Honeybun all had little presents for Mamma Cat, and they had put their pawprints on a pretty card.

     "What kind kittens you all are," said Mamma Cat, as her little ones crowded around her.

     Tiger Tail hid behind the chair. He had *meant* to remember. Quietly, he slipped out to buy a present.

Oh dear! Even when he was trying to do something good, Tiger Tail got into trouble. First he got caught on a thornbush and tore his trousers. Then, as he was looking over his shoulder to see whether his underpants were showing, he fell into a muddy puddle. And as he tried to clean himself up, the penny he had been clutching rolled out of his paw and fell into a little stream by the road.

It was late and beginning to get dark as Tiger Tail arrived home. Mamma Cat was waiting anxiously at the door as one tired and muddy little kitten threw himself into her arms and sobbed out the whole sorry story.

But Mamma Cat gave him a big kiss and squeezed him tight. "The best present of all is knowing that you are safe and sound, Tiger Tail," she said with a smile. "But what *have* you done to your trousers?"

The Great Escape

Lots of kittens like to collect something. It may be stamps, or shells, or leaves. At school, all the little kittens loved to show each other their latest finds.

"This is a very rare giant oyster shell," said Mopsy. "It might even have a pearl in it!"

"This is an even rarer triangle-shaped blue stamp from Gala-gala-land," said her friend Amybell.

"I've got a new dinosaur picture for my collection," said Honeybun. "It's a catosaurus!"

Even Tiger Tail, who preferred climbing trees to collecting things, had a very interesting box of feathers he'd found on his many fur-raising adventures.

Only George did not have a collection. It seemed that everything he was interested in was already collected by someone else. Then, one morning, as he was digging in the garden for his Granny, he had an idea. "There is one thing I am *really* interested in," he said to himself. "I'll start collecting today."

But George decided he would not tell anyone about his collection until it was really impressive. He kept it in his locker at school to keep it safe.

Unfortunately, George did not know that the lockers were cleaned every week. And the cleaner left his door ever so slightly open…

Next morning, Mrs Mumbles, the teacher, was busy showing the class some special number work when she suddenly gave a great shriek.

"Oooooh!" she cried. "Oooooooooh! Something slimy and slithery has squiggled down my neck!"

At the same moment, Mopsy jumped onto her desk. "Something wet and wiggly is sitting on my book!"

In no time at all, everyone was shouting at once. "The pencils are coming to life!" cried Honeybun, who always had a rather vivid imagination.

Only George was calm. "Stop!" he shouted. "You'll frighten them!"

At that moment, all the kittens and Mrs Mumbles stopped shouting and turned to look at George.

"It's just my collection," he explained. "They won't hurt you."

"I know I'm going to be sorry I asked you this, George," said Mrs Mumbles, "but what *exactly* did you collect?"

"Worms!" smiled George. "I had seventeen of them!"

It took *ages* for the class to find all the wriggly, wiggly worms. Can you find them any quicker?

143

Bella's Birthday

Most kittens are friendly and fun, but once in a while you may meet a kitten who is just a little too big for her boots. When Bella invited all the other kittens to her birthday party, she made sure they knew it would be the biggest and best party ever.

"I'm having a huge cake," she crowed. "And there will be giant balloons and a magician."

"It's a pity he can't make *her* disappear," whispered Rolypoly to Fluffy, "just for a while, anyway."

Bella lived in a very grand house, with columns either side of the door. When the kittens arrived, she greeted them in a dress that was so covered with ribbons and bows she could hardly move.

"Do come in," she said. "But please wipe your paws carefully. You poorer kittens may not be used to fine carpets."

Tiger Tail and Honeybun almost turned back right then, but they were curious about the magician and even more curious about the huge cake, so they joined their friends in the party room.

It would have been a lovely party, if Bella had not tried to show off at every opportunity. Even the magician, Mr Kat, got tired of her comments.

"I know how *that's* done," she said loudly, as he produced a bunch of flowers from a hat.

Mr Kat was tempted to ask Bella to take over, if she was so smart, but after all, it *was* her birthday.

"Now, listen to me!" called Bella, as everyone applauded at the end of the show. "Come into the garden, please, to watch me being photographed."

The kittens trooped outside, where Melinda Felini, the famous photographer, was waiting.

"Perhaps you'd like to hold these giant balloons, Bella," she suggested.

Bella grasped the bunch of balloons and smiled her widest smile … just as a gust of wind blew around the corner of the house. Up, up, and away went the birthday kitten!

Some say that Mr Kat used magic to make that wind blow. Some say that Melinda Felini had photographed Bella before and had not enjoyed it. Some say that Bella was a kind and quiet kitten ever after. But I believe I can hear her voice even now…

"Oh, haven't you tried ballooning, Mrs Mumbles? It's the *only* way to travel!"

The Package Problem

One autumn day, Mamma Cat really didn't feel too well. She sneezed and she sniffled as she sat in her chair.

"Don't worry, little ones," she said to her kittens. "It's only a cold, but I really don't think I should go outside today."

"No, no," said Mopsy. "You stay inside where it's warm and we'll do everything."

Mamma Cat looked a little doubtful. Last time the kittens had tried to help, she had spent three weeks putting things back in order. In fact, her knitting had been all tangled up ever since Honeybun had "finished" the sleeve of a sweater. But the little kittens looked so eager to help, and she did feel awful, so she agreed.

"I'll tell Fluffy and Rolypoly how to make dinner," she said. "Mopsy can make the beds, and Tiger Tail and Honeybun can take this package to Farmer Feather. It's his birthday."

Tiger Tail and Honeybun carried the package between them. It wasn't heavy, but it was an awkward shape. It was too far across for one little kitten to stretch his arms around it.

As soon as they got outside, the two kittens realized they had a big problem. The wind seemed to love that package! First it blew on it so hard that Tiger Tail and Honeybun could hardly hold on. Then they were pushed across the lane and into the hedge. As they came around the corner near Farmer Feather's farm, they found that the wind had somehow sneaked around behind them, and was blowing them past the farmhouse!

As they staggered into the barnyard, the wind played one last trick. It caught hold of the string on the package and wrapped it around the gatepost, so that it took Tiger Tail ten minutes to untangle it. (Honeybun never had been any good at untangling things, as Mamma Cat's knitting still showed!)

Farmer Feather was delighted with his present. It was too large to go through the doorway, so he opened it in the yard.

"Be careful," warned Honeybun. "The wind seems to want to play with it. It might fly away!"

But Farmer Feather laughed. "Oh no," he said. "The wind can play with it every day and it will never fly away. It's the most beautiful weather vane I've ever seen!"

Curious Kittens

Tiger Tail kicked at a leaf lying on the path. "I'm bored," he said. "We've played all our usual games."

The kittens were all outside on a beautiful sunny day, while Mamma Cat had some friends visiting.

"You kittens can stay outside," she had said, "so that we can have a little peace."

"Let's go down to Farmer Feather's farm," suggested Honeybun. "We can see what his weather vane looks like on the farmhouse."

So Mopsy poked her head through the doorway to tell Mamma Cat where they were going, and the five little kittens set off for the farm.

They came across Farmer Feather working on his tractor in a field before they reached the farmhouse. "Yes, you can go and look," he said, "but whatever you do, don't open the barn door."

Down at the farmhouse, the kittens thought the weather vane looked lovely.

"Now what?" asked Rolypoly. Tiger Tail didn't answer. He was looking at the barn.

The other kittens looked too.

"I wonder what is in there," said Rolypoly.

"So do I," said Fluffy.

"But we mustn't …" whispered Mopsy, "or at least, only very, very quickly."

Those five naughty kittens crept up to the barn door. They tried to peek in through the slats of wood, but they couldn't see anything.

"All right," said Rolypoly. "Let's open the door just a tiny, tiny bit."

Fluffy stood on tiptoes to open the latch. Then she pulled the door toward her ever so gently.

Squawk! Cluck! Quark! The kittens tumbled backward as twenty fluttering fowls rushed out of the barn.

There were hens everywhere, and just at that moment Farmer Feather came home. He was *not* happy.

"You kittens will just have to help me catch them," he said, rushing around the barnyard.

When they had finished, the kittens were out of breath but smiling. It had been great fun running after those skittering chickens. "Maybe we could let them out again sometime," giggled Honeybun.

Farmer Feather flopped down, panting. "Don't … even … *think* … about … it," he gasped.

The Pawprint Puzzle

For one whole week, the little kittens had been cooped up inside, while outside the wind blew and snow fell and the air was cold enough to freeze your whiskers.

While they were indoors, the kittens spent a lot of time pretending to be detectives. They solved the Mystery of the Missing Sock and the Puzzle of the Disappearing Pudding. Fluffy found her lost train set, and Honeybun found a lot of cobwebs in a cupboard.

At last Mamma Cat looked out and said, "The snow has stopped, and the sun is shining. Put on your mittens and go outside."

Tiger Tail was ready first. He slipped out of the back door with a smile. "Come and find me when you're ready!" he called.

When the other little kittens opened the front door, Tiger Tail was nowhere to be seen. The kittens called, but there was no answer. Where could he have gone?

"I know," said Honeybun. "We can be detectives again and follow his pawprints in the snow!" A nice clear set of prints led away from the back door. They led down the path and up to the gate. And there they stopped. All around, the snow was smooth and gleaming white.

"He must have opened the gate," said Fluffy. But the gate had not been disturbed.

"Maybe he jumped over," said Rolypoly. But there were no footprints at all on the other side of the gate – or anywhere else!

At last Mopsy made an important announcement. "If he didn't go through, or over, or along … he went up!"

Four little kittens looked up at the blue sky. There were no clouds. There were no planes. There were no balloons, or kites, or gliders. There most definitely was no Tiger Tail.

At that moment, they heard a giggling sound. It was Tiger Tail!

"Foiled again, great detectives!" he chortled. "It's simple. I walked to the gate, and then I walked back again … backward! I put my paws in the prints I'd made before. Ha! Ha!"

Splat! A snowball hit Tiger Tail on the nose, and for the next half-hour, the great detectives had lots of fun taking their revenge!

The Picnic Pie

One sunny day, Mamma Cat had a surprise for the little kittens. "We're all going into the woods for a picnic," she said. "And if you will make some sandwiches, I will make a special pie for us."

"Can it be a cherry pie, Mamma?" asked Tiger Tail. "Cherry pie is what I like best, even if it does make my whiskers pink!"

"Oh no, Mamma," chorused Fluffy and Honeybun. "We like apple pie best. There are two of us, so it should be apple."

"There are two of us, too," cried Mopsy and Rolypoly, "and we like plum pie best."

"What am I going to do with you?" sighed Mamma Cat. "We'll ask your father what he likes best, and that is what we'll have. Then there will be no arguments."

At that moment, Father Cat came in from the garden with a basket of fruit.

"Daddy," cried Mopsy, "what kind of pie do you like best? Mamma says she'll make it!"

Father Cat smiled at Mamma Cat. "What a treat," he said. "Well, I don't mind. Whatever you like, sweetheart. All your pies are delicious!"

"Then I will decide," said Mamma Cat. "You kittens can start making the sandwiches, and you, Father Cat, can find the picnic basket."

An hour later, the picnic was ready. The sandwiches were packed in boxes and put in the basket. And sitting on top of everything, looking and smelling wonderful, was an enormous picnic pie. But Mamma Cat wouldn't tell anyone what she had put in it.

"You'll find out soon enough," she said.

It was lovely walking through the trees and even nicer when they sat down to munch their sandwiches. Then it was time for the famous pie. Mamma Cat cut slices for everyone and handed them out on paper plates.

"Just don't say anything until you've tasted it," she said.

Tiger Tail took a bite. "It *is* cherry!" he cried. "Thank you, Mamma."

"But there are some apples in it too," grinned Fluffy and Honeybun.

"And plums," shouted Mopsy and Rolypoly.

"It's a mixed-fruit pie," smiled Mamma. "There's something for everyone."

"You know," said Father Cat with his mouth full, "I've just remembered. *This* is the kind of pie I like best!"

153

It's a Monster!

There are lots of exciting things to do at school, but sometimes those naughty little kittens just didn't want to do as they were told. One day, Mrs Mumbles, their teacher, asked them to do some reading practice, but the kittens really didn't want to sit still and read.

After lots of interruptions, Mrs Mumbles rolled up her sleeves and pretended to look very serious. "Now," she said, "while you read your books, I must straighten out the supply room."

"No, no!" cried the kittens. "We can do it!" They had secretly all wanted to find out what was kept behind the supply room door.

"All right," said Mrs Mumbles uncertainly. "But there are all kinds of things in there, so I want you little kittens to be very, very careful. Some supplies can be dangerous."

The kittens looked surprised. Dangerous? What could there be that would be dangerous?

"Maybe there are kitten-eating spiders in there," whispered Bella. "I'd better stay out here."

"There might be something old and green," suggested George, whose mother was always warning him about leaving half-eaten cakes under his bed. "It would be very smelly and…"

"Yes, yes," interrupted Honeybun quickly. "But I've thought of something even worse it might be. It might be … *a monster*!"

"They do often live in small dark places," agreed Tiger Tail. "We're going to have to be very, very careful."

So the bravest kittens – Tiger Tail, Mopsy, and George – crept into the supply room. It was very dark, and huge piles of books and equipment towered overhead. As they reached the back of the tiny room, George fell over a bucket. A mop and a swimming towel went flying, and an old drum went BOOM!

The three brave kittens had never run so fast in their lives. "It *is* a monster!" they shouted. "It's got floppy hair and flappy arms and it goes BOOM! Shut the door quick!"

Mrs Mumbles came along to find a whole class of kittens reading very nicely from their books. She gave a small smile to herself. Well, well. So the mop-and-bucket monster trick had worked again this year!

Now Remember...

Mamma Cat looked at the clock. She knew that she had to mail her letters now or it would be too late. But Father Cat wasn't home yet and Honeybun, Rolypoly, Tiger Tail, and Mopsy were playing on the floor.

"I just don't know what to do," said Mamma Cat. "It's very important that these letters are sent today."

"We'll be all right, Mamma," said Mopsy. "Daddy will be home soon, and we will be good."

"Well, I suppose you are old enough to take care of yourselves for a few minutes," Mamma Cat agreed. "But you must promise that you won't open the door for anyone, except Father, of course."

"We promise!" said the kittens. So Mamma Cat put on her coat and hurried off to the post office.

She had only been gone for a few minutes when there was a tapping at the door.

"Let me in! Let me in!" called a little voice.

It was Fluffy, who had just come home from her piano lesson. The front door could only be opened from the inside.

The kittens looked at each other. "We promised not to open the door," said Rolypoly anxiously, "except for Daddy."

"But it's starting to rain," cried Mopsy. "Poor Fluffy will get wet, and you know how long it takes to dry *her* fur!"

"But we promised…" Rolypoly was so upset he was almost crying.

Then Tiger Tail had one of his Good Ideas. "We promised not to open the door," he said, "but we didn't promise anything *at all* about the window!"

And that is why, when Mamma Cat and Father Cat arrived home at almost the same moment a little while later, they found Fluffy's little legs waving out of the window, where she was well and truly stuck!

Poor Fluffy was soon rescued, and the little kittens explained what had happened. For a moment they thought that Mamma Cat was going to be angry, but then she smiled.

"Poor little kittens," she said. "All the time I was telling you to *remember* your promise, I'd *forgotten* something very important myself. It's a good thing I stopped at the bakery on the way home to get you a treat."

Mamma Cat had bought some delicious pastries for everyone.

"And Fluffy can choose first," laughed Tiger Tail, "as long as she doesn't choose the cherry bun!"

The Treehouse

Most little kittens love to climb trees. They can't resist finding out what they can see from the highest branches, even if they do wave and wiggle in the wind. But climbing down trees is a different matter. That is something that kittens prefer not to do, which is why they so often get stuck.

The little kittens loved to visit the woods and climb the highest trees, but after the fifth time he was called out to make a daring rescue, Father Cat put his paw down.

"You kittens are just going to have to find some other way to have fun in the woods," he said. "One day I may be away when you need rescuing. Now I must go back to the house. Farmer Feather is lending me his ladder so that I can fix the roof."

There was something about the word "ladder" that gave Mopsy the tingling feeling that often means a Really Good Idea is about to arrive.

"Quiet!" she called. "I need quiet! Let me think."

The kittens knew what that meant. Mopsy's brain cells were working overtime, and they must keep out of the way.

The kittens did not have to wait long. Mopsy's whiskers began to wiggle. Her ears twitched. Her bright little eyes sparkled.

"She's got an idea!" cried Rolypoly, who knew the signs.

"We," said Mopsy grandly, "are going to build a treehouse."

It was such a Really Good Idea that the other little kittens didn't hesitate. They set off at once for Farmer Feather's wood-shed to … well … *borrow* some of Farmer Feather's wood.

Considering that five little architects helped with the plans, and five little builders hoisted and hammered, and five little painters splished and sploshed, the treehouse was finished in an amazingly short time. It did look unlike any other treehouse you have ever seen, to be sure, but it was snug, and cheerful, and in a tree – what more could a kitten wish for?

The little kittens have decided to keep the treehouse a secret for now, but Father Cat is already very suspicious about the painty pawprints on his path. He wonders if they could have anything to do with the mysterious disappearance of Farmer Feather's ladder…

Oh, Pickles!

One morning, Mamma Cat received a letter. "Your cousin Pickles is coming to stay," she said, looking at her own five little kittens.

There was silence for a moment.

"Over my dead body!" cried Father Cat, leaping to his feet. "Do you remember last time? I had to replumb the bathroom, retile the kitchen, put up a new fence, and apologize to all the cats for miles around for things that kitten had done. I'm not going through all that again."

The little kittens agreed.

They liked their cousin, but it was pretty risky having him to stay.

"I'm afraid we don't have much choice," said Mamma Cat. "My sister is really not well. Someone must take care of Pickles. Besides, this letter was mailed a week ago. He's already on his way."

"Then we must batten down the hatches," said Father Cat grimly, "and get ready."

The kittens took him at his word. They hid their nicest toys and put anything that was breakable well out of reach.

"That's going too far!" laughed Mamma Cat, when Father Cat came in wearing an old army helmet. "He's not that bad!"

And the funny thing was that Pickles was not bad at all. He was polite to his uncle and aunt and he sat down at the table as meekly as any kitten you have ever seen.

"Well, Pickles," said Father Cat. "You really seem to have changed. You … er … certainly made your presence felt last time you were here."

"Oh, " smiled Pickles. "I was little then. I'm much more grown up now. Thank you for a lovely dinner. I think I'll go to bed early after my trip."

Pickles stood up and turned away. Unfortunately, the tablecloth had been tucked in his belt. In one quick motion, the plates, the saucers, the casserole, and Mamma Cat's famous marmalade pudding went hurtling across the room.

"Oh, Pickles!" cried Father Cat, Mamma Cat, and the five kittens, with tears of laughter rolling down their cheeks. "You haven't changed at all!"

Ssssh!

One night, when all the kittens and their parents were fast asleep, Tiger Tail woke up with a start. He was sure that he had heard something. Maybe it was burglars! He crept bravely out of bed and went to investigate. But as Tiger Tail went out into the hallway, the bedroom door closed with a loud *click*!

The next thing Tiger Tail knew, Fluffy was creeping along the hallway too.

"I thought I heard a noise like a *click*," she whispered.

"That was me," said Tiger Tail. "Ssssh!"

But Fluffy had already knocked an apple out of the fruit bowl. It fell with a *thud*!

Seconds later, Rolypoly tiptoed out into the hallway to meet them.

"I thought I heard a kind of *thud*," he said.

"That was me," said Fluffy. "Ssssh!"

But Rolypoly had already bumped into a bookshelf. A book fell over with a *wumph*!

Almost at once, Mopsy crept out to join the other kittens.

"I thought I heard a sort of *wumph* noise," she whispered.

"That was me," said Rolypoly. "Ssssh!"

But Rolypoly didn't notice his father's shoes standing by the door. One of them went skidding across the floor and hit the wall with a *thwack*!

Honeybun came creeping along to join them.

"I thought I heard a *thwack*!" he hissed.

"That was me," said Rolypoly. "Ssssh!"

But Honeybun had slipped on the mat. He fell over with a *thump*!

Mamma Cat came hurrying out of her room.

"I thought I heard a *thump*," she said.

"That was me," replied Honeybun. "Ssssh!"

They all listened. There was a very quiet munching sound coming from the kitchen.

"Follow me," said Mamma Cat, picking up an umbrella.

She flung open the kitchen door. There sat Father Cat, with a huge sandwich.

"Just a little midnight snack!" he cried guiltily.

"Ssssh!" said the brave burglar-beaters. "We're trying to *sleep*, you know!"

The Lost Letter

One wet morning, Honeybun could not find the hood for his raincoat. "The other kittens had better start out for school without you," said Mamma Cat. "You can catch up with them when you find your hood. It must be around here somewhere."

Five minutes later, the kitten found his missing hood.

"You won't be late if you hurry," said Mamma Cat.

As Honeybun was running down the lane, he met the mailcat, Mr String.

"I've got a letter for your mother," said Mr String. "Will you take it for her?"

Honeybun took the letter and carefully put it in his pocket. He would give it to Mamma Cat that afternoon after school.

But when he came home from school that day, Honeybun forgot all about the letter. As luck would have it, the weather was sunny for ages afterward. It was about six weeks later that Honeybun put on his raincoat again and felt the paper crinkling under his paw.

The kitten felt dreadful. What if it was something important? He took the letter out of his pocket and read the big red writing on the front. "YOU ARE A WINNER!" it said. "CLAIM NOW OR LOSE YOUR PRIZE!"

Honeybun felt sick. He imagined the huge amount of money that his carelessness might have lost. Or maybe it was a car! Or a trip to the sunshine! His family would never forgive him.

Honeybun panicked. Maybe no one ever had to know. He hid the letter and went to school.

But all day Honeybun felt awful. It was as if he had a heavy weight in his tummy.

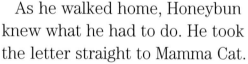

As he walked home, Honeybun knew what he had to do. He took the letter straight to Mamma Cat.

"I'm sorry," he sobbed, as he explained.

Mamma Cat put her arm around her little one. "It was just a mistake, honey," she said. "Let's see what this silly thing is about."

Honeybun couldn't understand why Mamma Cat laughed and laughed when she read the letter.

"Well done, Honeybun," she said, between giggles. "We would have won a lifetime's supply of Purple Fizz, and you know how we all hate that yucky drink. You saved us from being purple fizzily flooded!"

Who's Who?

The little kittens had gone to see an exciting movie. When they got home, they could only think of one thing.

"Let's play spies!" suggested Tiger Tail.

"We'll need to disguise ourselves," said Mopsy.

So the five little kittens went off to find disguises.

One of the kittens found a sheet, a pillowcase, and an old belt.

"I'm going to disguise myself as an Arab sheik," he said, putting on some dark glasses.

Another little kitten crept into Mamma Cat's bedroom. She found a huge hat, and a coat, and some shoes.

"I'm a lady of mystery," she said, pulling down the veil of the hat.

The third little kitten went to Father Cat's chest of drawers. He found some trousers, and a jacket, and an old-fashioned hat.

"I'm a double agent," he said. And he put on his dark glasses.

In Mamma Cat's sewing box, another little kitten found some beautiful silk fabric. She wound it around herself.

"I'm a princess from India," she said, pulling the silk across her nose.

The last little kitten couldn't decide what disguise to wear. Then he saw Father Cat's coveralls on the washing machine. He put a scarf over his nose and a helmet on his head.

"I'm a racing driver," he said.

The kittens had a wonderful time playing spies that afternoon, until Mamma Cat and Father Cat came home from shopping.

"Who's been in my room, borrowing my clothes?" cried Mamma Cat.

"And who's been in my chest of drawers, borrowing my clothes?" yelled Father Cat.

"And someone's been in my sewing basket too," said Mamma Cat.

"And my coveralls are missing," said Father Cat.

They soon found five very guilty-looking spies.

"It's lucky you spies are in disguise," said Father Cat, trying not to smile. "If I knew which of you was which, I'd have to give you a serious talking-to."

The little kittens scampered off to put their disguises away. I'll bet *you* could tell which was which, couldn't you? But don't tell Father Cat!

Huggie's Hat

All the little kittens loved to visit Farmer Feather's farm. There were so many different things to see and do there. And, of course, there was Huggie, too.

Huggie had worked for Farmer Feather for more years than the little kittens could count. He knew everything there was to know about growing crops and looking after animals. The kittens loved to hear his stories about life on the farm years ago, and they liked watching Huggie work as well.

One day, Huggie greeted them with a smile and a wave.

"I've got a job for you little kittens today," he said. "We need a new scarecrow in the top field. I thought you might want to make him for me. Here are some sticks to make him stand up straight. You can fill these sacks with straw to make his head and body, and here are some old clothes to dress him in when you're finished. Have fun!"

The kittens loved making the scarecrow. Honeybun had some crayons in his pocket, so they drew a happy face on the scarecrow's head. They made sure that they put lots of straw in his tummy so he looked fat and jolly.

It wasn't easy dressing the scarecrow. He seemed as wriggly as a baby kitten. When they were finished, the kittens looked at their creation.

"Something about him isn't right," said Tiger Tail.

"His legs are too thin," said Mopsy. "Let's stuff them with straw. We can tie the bottoms with string."

When the scarecrow's legs were fatter, he looked just right. Huggie came in to have a look.

"That's wonderful," he said, scratching his head. "He looks a little like me! Now you can take him into the middle of the field and push him into the ground."

But Fluffy was still frowning after Huggie had left.

"There's something missing," she said. "He needs a hat!"

"There wasn't a hat with the clothes," said Tiger Tail.

Then all the kittens noticed that Huggie had left his battered old hat behind. It was perfect!

Later that afternoon, the scarecrow watched as the kittens started out for home.

"See you again soon," called Huggie. "You haven't seen my hat anywhere, have you?"

169

A Fishy Tale

One late summer day, Honeybun decided to go down to the river to see if anything exciting was happening there. But when he mentioned it at breakfast, Mamma Cat put her paw down.

"Water is dangerous," she said, "even for young kittens who are good swimmers. You must never go down to the river without a grown-up cat. And that goes for you others, too."

Honeybun was really disappointed. It was just the kind of sunny, breezy, soft day when it is fun to be near the water.

Just then, he saw Farmer Feather going past in the lane. He was dressed rather strangely and carrying a long pole. Honeybun forgot about the river and ran out to see where his friend was going.

"I'm off to the river to do some fishing," said Farmer Feather. "Would you like to come, too?"

Honeybun couldn't believe his furry little ears. He ran inside to tell Mamma right away.

"As long as you stay with Farmer Feather, that's fine," she said. "Bring us back a fish for our supper!"

Honeybun skipped along the road beside Farmer Feather, but the older cat shook his head.

"I don't want any skipping and jumping when we're near the river, young kitten. You'll frighten the fish away!"

They soon reached the riverbank. Farmer Feather set up his fishing rod and a large green umbrella. Then he reeled out his line and sat down.

Honeybun sat down, too. "What happens now?" he asked.

"We wait," said the farmer. "Ssssh!"

Honeybun waited for *ages*.

"Now what do we do?"

"We wait some more. Sssh!"

Honeybun waited as long as he could.

"If you don't stop wriggling, you'll have to go home," said Farmer Feather.

"How much longer do we have to wait?" asked Honeybun.

"Who knows? An hour or two? Or three? Or four?"

Honeybun sat still for a moment. "I've just remembered something very important I've got to do," he said.

"What, no fish?" called Mamma Cat, later at home.

"It was hopeless," said Honeybun. "Farmer Feather kept *talking*, and he scared them all away!"

The Squiggly Thing

One morning, Rolypoly pushed his bowl away at breakfast. That wasn't like him at all!

"What's the matter, Rolypoly?" asked Mamma Cat.

"I don't want it," said Rolypoly.

"Why not?" Mamma Cat felt her son's furry forehead. "Do you feel sick?"

"Noooo," said Rolypoly slowly. "I'm all right."

"What is it, then?" asked Mamma.

"Can I whisper?" asked the little kitten.

So Rolypoly climbed onto Mamma Cat's lap and whispered in her ear. He didn't want the other little kittens to hear.

"I've got a squiggly thing in my tummy!" he said.

"A squiggly thing?" said Mamma. "What have you been eating, Rolypoly?" She carried the kitten over to the window where they could talk quietly.

"Nothing," whispered her son. "It's just a very wriggly, squiggly thing."

Mamma Cat looked at him carefully.

"Is it wriggling and squiggling all the time?" she asked.

"No," said Rolypoly, "only when I think about my reading test."

Then Mamma Cat understood. Some of the little kittens had a reading test at school that morning, and it was making Rolypoly nervous. The squiggly thing was just nervousness in his tummy.

"But Rolypoly," said Mamma, "you read beautifully. You haven't been worried before, have you?"

"No, but Tiger Tail told me that this was a Really Important Test and he has been feeling terribly worried about it."

Mamma Cat looked across at Tiger Tail.

"He doesn't look very worried to me," she said. "He's got marmalade all over his whiskers and butter on his paws. I think Tiger Tail has been very naughty to make you so worried. I will talk to him later. Now, Rolypoly, you just do your best on the test. That's all you can possibly do. And I will be proud of you no matter how you do."

Then Mamma Cat gave Rolypoly a big hug, and the little kitten found that the squiggly thing had wriggled right away.

That afternoon, the little kittens were all cheering Rolypoly when they came home from school.

"He got the highest mark," said Mopsy. "Isn't that good?"

"That's wonderful!" said Mamma Cat. "And how did Tiger Tail do?"

"Not very well," said Mopsy. "I think he's hiding."

"I'll find him," said Mamma Cat. "I need to have words with that young kitten." Can you find him first?

Alfred to the Rescue

One morning, the little kittens were playing outside, while Mamma Cat sat in the sunshine and shelled some peas. Father Cat had borrowed Farmer Feather's new ladder (he had lost his old one around the time the kittens built their treehouse) to paint the upstairs windows.

Just then, a little kitten went past in the lane and waved to Mamma Cat's family. The kittens ignored him.

"Who was that?" asked Mamma Cat.

"Oh," said Fluffy, "that was Alfred. He's new at school."

"Why didn't you ask him to come and play?" asked Mamma. "He looked like a nice little kitten to me."

"Oh, he wouldn't want to play with us," said Tiger Tail. "The teacher is always saying how smart he is."

"Well, all my kittens are smart in their own ways," said Mamma Cat. "I hope you're not being unkind. I thought Alfred looked a little lonely."

Half an hour later, the kittens were playing an exciting game of chase-the-tail.

"Careful!" warned Father Cat, high up on his ladder. "You almost made me wobble!"

But Tiger Tail, tearing around the corner of the house, didn't hear him.

Crash! He knocked the ladder sideways. Father Cat lost his footing. As he grabbed the top of the window, his paint can sailed up into the air and down again, landing on his head.

"Help!" cried Father Cat. "I can't see a thing!"

"Help!" cried Mamma Cat. "What can we do?"

"Help!" cried the little kittens. "He's going to fall."

"Keep calm!" cried a voice from the lane. It was Alfred, and he took charge at once.

"I'm going to talk you down, Mr Cat," he said. "Just do exactly what I say. Now move your right paw a little to the left...."

In next to no time, Alfred had saved the day. Everyone was so happy that Father Cat was safe that they didn't scold the little kittens. But everyone wanted to congratulate Alfred and be his friend.

"I'm just glad you weren't hurt, Mr Cat," said Alfred.

"Not hurt," giggled Mamma Cat, "but a lovely shade of lavender. It's very becoming, dear!"

Aunt Amelia

Mamma Cat was surprised when Mrs Mumbles stopped her in the street one Saturday morning. Mrs Mumbles was the little kittens' schoolteacher.

"I was just wondering, Mrs Cat," said Mrs Mumbles in sympathetic tones, "how your dear sister is now. The kittens have been so worried about her. I do understand that they find it hard to concentrate in class when she is on their minds."

"My sister?" said Mamma faintly.

"Yes," said Mrs Mumbles, "the kittens' Aunt Amelia. I do hope there is good news."

"Excellent news," said Mamma Cat briskly. "She has made a remarkable recovery and went home this morning. I'm glad to say that the kittens don't need to worry anymore. In fact, I'm sure they will want to work extra hard next week to catch up on their work."

"I can help them with that," said Mrs Mumbles. "Do tell your sister how glad I am that she's better. Good-bye!"

"Good-bye!" said Mamma Cat. "I will!" And that, you know, was very strange, because although Mamma Cat has six brothers, she has no sisters at all.

But while Mamma Cat was walking home, she decided that maybe she *did* have a sister after all. She walked home and beamed at her kittens, who were trying to do acrobatics on the grass.

"My dears," said Mamma, "I have wonderful news! Your Aunt Amelia, who has been so ill, is much better now and is coming to stay with us!"

The kittens looked at each other. They knew perfectly well that Tiger Tail and Honeybun had invented Aunt Amelia on the spur of the moment when they were faced with an extra-long spelling test. Since then, she had become very useful indeed. But what did Mamma mean? How could a make-believe aunt come to stay?"

"Oh, Mamma," said Mopsy. "I don't understand. How *can* Aunt Amelia visit?"

"Well, why shouldn't she?" asked Mamma

"Well … because … because …" Honeybun didn't quite know how to begin.

"Because there isn't a real Aunt Amelia," said Tiger Tail. "We made her up, Mamma. I'm sorry."

"I know," said Mamma. "And if you naughty little kittens aren't *very* good over the next few weeks, Mrs Mumbles will know too."

"We'll be good!" chorused the little kittens. After all, Mrs Mumbles is a very intelligent cat, who knows a very great deal, but she doesn't need to know *everything*!

Katie's Clock

Mamma Cat did her best to make sure that her little kittens were never late for school. She kept a sharp eye on the clock in the mornings.

Unfortunately, Katie Kitten, who lived next door, was nearly always late. Her mother had not five but twelve little kittens to look after. It was not surprising that she often forgot to wind the clock, so it nearly always showed the wrong time.

After a while, Mrs Mumbles lost patience with poor Katie.

"Katie Kitten!" she said. "You are late again. Don't you have a watch?"

"No, Mrs Mumbles," said Katie.

"Oh," said Mrs Mumbles, "well, please try to be more punctual in the future."

Next morning, Katie was not just on time – she was early!

"I've got something better than a watch," she smiled, "but it's a secret."

For the rest of that week, Katie was on time. Mrs Mumbles was very pleased.

The following Monday, Katie was at school bright and early again. That morning, Mrs Mumbles gave the class a multiplication test.

"I want absolute silence," she said.

But it seemed that absolute silence was difficult to find. First one of Farmer Feather's noisiest tractors rumbled slowly by in the lane. Then a dog trotted by, barking loudly.

"Don't be distracted, class," said Mrs Mumbles. "Hopefully, we'll have peace now."

But just then … *drriiiiiiing! drriiiiiiing! drriiiiiiing!* Mrs Mumbles nearly jumped out of her fur. She looked around the class. One little kitten was looking very pink. It was Katie.

"I'm sorry," she said. "I've been bringing my Granny's alarm clock, so that I'm not late."

"Katie," said Mrs Mumbles, "You are not to bring an alarm clock to school again."

That evening, the kittens told Mamma Cat what had happened. Later, when they were in bed, Mamma Cat left Father Cat in charge and slipped out on an errand, carrying a small box.

Much to the kittens' surprise, Katie was on time again the next morning.

"Look!" she said. "A surprise present came through the door last night. It's a watch! I wish I knew where it came from."

I think that's our secret, don't you?

Splish! Splash!

Mamma Cat sighed as she looked at the dirty dishes by the sink. "Oh dear," she groaned, "I do *hate* washing dishes!"

"We'll do it for you, Mamma," said Mopsy, ignoring nudges from Tiger Tail on one side and Rolypoly on the other.

"Are you sure you can manage?" asked Mamma, looking surprised and a little anxious.

Mopsy tried to look grown up and sensible. "Of course we can," she said.

Mamma Cat was very tired, so she stopped listening to the little warning voice in her head. She went into the living room and put her paws up. Soon she was fast asleep.

Reluctantly, Fluffy and Rolypoly cleared the rest of the dishes from the kitchen table. Tiger Tail took charge of the sink … and turned on the water so hard that everyone was soaked. Meanwhile, Mopsy squeezed just a little too much dishwashing liquid into the sink.

"What lovely bubbles!" squealed Fluffy. "We could have a bubble-blowing contest!"

For ten minutes, the dishwashing was forgotten as five little kittens chased bubbles around the kitchen. By the time they'd finished, they had to squeeze more bubbles into the sink because the others were used up.

At last Honeybun began washing the dishes. Fluffy and Mopsy dried, and Rolypoly and Tiger Tail put the cups, plates, knives, forks, and spoons away.

The floor was fairly slippery by now, with all the spilled water and bubbles, so it wasn't really Rolypoly's fault when he fell over and a few things got broken.

When everything was put away, Tiger Tail said, "There's still lots of bubbly water. What do you think we should do with it?" It did seem a shame to waste it, so he and Mopsy ran upstairs to find their bath toys.

When Mamma Cat came in a few minutes later, she suddenly felt much more tired than she had before.

"We can't understand why you don't like washing dishes, Mamma," cried the five little kittens. "We think it's lots of fun!"

The Pumpkin Prize

For weeks, Father Cat had a determined look on his face. "This year," he said, "I'm going to do it. Oh yes."

"Does it really matter?" asked Mamma Cat. "It's only a little prize."

"It's not the prize. It's the principle," said Father Cat sternly, reaching for his watering can.

It was the time of year when the local Fruit and Vegetable Show was only weeks away. For more years than he cared to remember, Father Cat had tried to win the Pumpkin Prize. It was for the biggest, roundest, brightest orange pumpkin in the show. And for just as many years, the biggest, roundest, brightest orange pumpkin had been grown by Farmer Feather. Father Cat and Farmer Feather were the best of friends, but at this time of year, they only muttered to each other as they passed. They were deadly rivals.

This year, the kittens had bought Father Cat a special book for his birthday. It was called *Expert Pumpkin Growing*. There was only one problem. Father Cat wasn't an expert. He couldn't understand the book, which was full of the longest words he had ever seen.

Maybe just owning the book was enough, for that year Father Cat managed to grow a really huge orange pumpkin.

Long before the show, he realized that his wheelbarrow would not be big enough to carry it, so he made a special little cart.

On the morning of the show, the little kittens and Mamma Cat all gathered to help Father Cat load the pumpkin.

"Left a bit. Right a bit. Careful!" called Father Cat, as the pumpkin was rolled onto the cart. It was much too heavy to lift.

"I'll open the gate," said Honeybun, running down the path.

But opening the gate did not help. The pumpkin was much wider than the cart or the gate. It just would not go through.

"Oh dear, what a shame," said Father Cat. "It would probably have won the prize, but it will have to stay in the garden. Never mind."

Mamma Cat and the little kittens couldn't believe that Father Cat was taking it all so well. But then, they hadn't seen what he had just seen, far away in one of Farmer Feather's fields, had they?

The Christmas Kittens

It was the coldest, snowiest Christmas Mamma and Father Cat could remember. The little kittens loved it. They made snowcats and had snowball fights. Then, when the light began to fade in the afternoon and even their whiskers felt a little frosty, they would hurry inside for hot chocolate and one of Mamma Cat's special little mince pies.

"This is perfect weather for Christmas," sighed Fluffy, gazing out of the window at the best snowcat she had made yet. "And there are only three days to go!" She couldn't keep a little squeak of excitement out of her voice.

"I'd rather be staying with my cousin Fred in Australia," muttered Father Cat, who had had enough of clearing snow from the path and getting icicles in his ears. "He'll be sitting on the beach in the sunshine on Christmas Day, *and* he'll have warm ears!"

"You know," said Mamma Cat, "we are very lucky to have such a nice, warm home at Christmastime, even if it is cold outside. Some cats and kittens are not so lucky. I think we should ask another family to join us on Christmas Day, to share our dinner."

"No!" said Father Cat. "Five little kittens squealing over their presents and getting tired and tearful are enough!"

"No!" said Mopsy. "Strange kittens might break my new toys."

"No!" said Rolypoly. "Other kittens would eat *my* little mince pie."

"No!" said Tiger Tail. "If we have visitors, we'll have to be *quiet*."

"No!" said Honeybun. "It's fun with just us here."

"Well," said Fluffy, "I'm not sure it would be fun if we were thinking about poor little kittens who aren't so lucky all the time."

"We wouldn't be," said Mopsy.

"I would," sighed Fluffy.

"So would I," said Mamma Cat.

"Well, if you put it like that…" muttered Father Cat.

"I suppose there *are* enough mince pies," said Rolypoly.

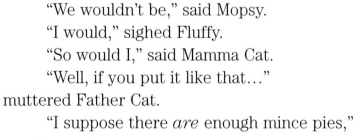

So that was why there were *eleven* little kittens around the Christmas table that year. And those kittens *did* get tired and tearful. And Mopsy's new bicycle *did* get broken (and fixed again by Father Cat). And *all* the mince pies were eaten. And Tiger Tail was not at all quiet. And everyone had the best Christmas *ever*!

A New Friend

The little kittens were not very happy when they heard that Great Aunt Florence was coming to stay.

"Remember," said Mamma Cat, "Great Aunt Florence is not a young cat. She will need peace and quiet more than anything else. There must be no shouting, Rolypoly. No running around, Tiger Tail. No squealing, Fluffy. No talking with your mouth full, Rolypoly. And no yelling, Mopsy. Do you understand?"

"Yes, Mamma," said the little kittens, but they could feel their whiskers drooping. They imagined a very old, frail cat sitting in a chair with a shawl around her shoulders and a blanket around her knees. There would be no fun in the house at all while she was staying.

But when Great Aunt Florence arrived, she wasn't at all like they had expected.

"Great Aunt Florence is such a mouthful," she said. "Call me Flo!"

Flo wore lots and lots of beads and bangles. (And they sometimes dangled in her soup!)

Flo wore extraordinary clothes with frills and flounces. (And they sometimes got caught on the door handles!)

Flo spoke in a loud voice and used words that made Father Cat shudder and the little kittens giggle!

Still, the little kittens remembered what Mamma had said, and they tried hard to be good and quiet. They did their very best for three days, before Tiger Tail said, "I can't stand this anymore. Let's go right to the end of the orchard, where no one can hear us, and have a good game of soccer. I might burst if I can't shout and run around."

The other little kittens didn't need persuading. In less than a minute they were under the apple trees, having a really exciting game.

When Great Aunt Florence appeared suddenly from behind a flower bed, the kittens felt a little ashamed. They had been very noisy. But Flo had a sparkle in her eye.

"Well, well, soccer!" she cried. "I was beginning to worry about you kittens. You were so good and quiet."

She took off her big hat and tossed it into a tree.

Flo expertly kicked the ball right at her hat. "GOAL!" she yelled. "Catch me if you can!"

A Terrible Tangle

Mamma Cat was knitting squares as if her life depended on it. They were very small squares, and the little kittens were all very puzzled by them.

"Maybe they're blankets for baby rabbits," said Mopsy, who had been reading a story about bunnies.

"They could be dishcloths," said Rolypoly, looking bored.

"No one," said Fluffy, "could need so many dishcloths. I think they're little shawls for dolls."

Mamma Cat looked up and smiled. "The squares are going to be joined together," she said, "to make a big bright blanket. I'm making one, and Mrs Willow is making one. I'm determined to finish first."

The little kittens didn't like Mrs Willow much.

"Let us help you, Mamma!" said Fluffy. "You're sure to win then."

Mamma looked a little doubtful, but the kittens looked so eager, she agreed at last.

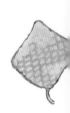

"I'm using yarn from some old sweaters you've outgrown," she said. "All you have to do is unravel them by pulling gently, like this, and wind the yarn into little balls."

"We can do that!" cried the kittens. It looked like fun.

"I'll just go and put dinner in the oven," said Mamma Cat. "Just call me if you need help."

But the little kittens were enjoying themselves too much to call when things began to go ever so slightly wrong. When Mamma Cat walked back into the room, she couldn't believe the sight that met her eyes. Bright yarn was crisscrossing the room in all directions. It was hanging from the lamp and twirling around the furniture.

"Oh no!" groaned Mamma Cat.

But when Tiger Tail saw how upset Mamma was, he had a good idea.

"There will be a special prize," he announced, "for the kitten who winds up all of his or her ball first."

Who do you think won? And who is in danger of undoing all of Mamma's hard work?

What's My Name?

One evening, Mamma Cat read the little kittens a story they had never heard before. It was about a funny little man who helped a girl marry the King. In return, he asked for her first baby. Of course, when the time came, the Queen did not want to give up her baby. The little man told her that he would disappear forever if she could guess his name. You probably know this story already. It is called "Rumpelstiltskin".

The next day, the little kittens were still thinking about the story.

"It was lucky the Queen managed to find out the name," said Mopsy. "She would never have been able to guess it."

"Nonsense!" cried Tiger Tail. "I bet I could have guessed it. You could see from the pictures that the little man looked just like someone who would be called Rumpelstiltskin."

"Is that so?" asked Mamma Cat. "So you wouldn't have any trouble guessing your *father's* name then?"

"But we know his name," said Fluffy. "It's Charles."

"Yes," said Mamma Cat. "But his full name is Charles F. Cat. Do you know what the *F* stands for?"

"Now, now, we don't need to go into that," muttered Father Cat from behind his newspaper.

But the little kittens were curious now.

"Is it Ferdinand, Frederick, Francis, or Felix?" they asked.

"No," said Father Cat.

"Is it Finton, Felipe, Forrest, or Fingle?" asked the kittens.

"No," said Father Cat.

"Is it Floozle, Fenugreek, Fandangle, or Finklefog?" asked Tiger Tail.

"*No!*" cried Father Cat.

For days, the kittens tried to guess. They spent more time with their encyclopedias and dictionaries than Mrs Mumbles their teacher had ever been able to persuade them to do before. At last, after the fifth dinnertime at which Father Cat had been bombarded with very unlikely-sounding names beginning with *F*, he put his paw down.

"There will be no more guessing about my name," he said. "It's a very silly name. My parents were just not concentrating at the time. I have no intention of telling you … ever!"

"Now, dear," said Mamma Cat. "I think it's a sweet name. After all, you did use it for one of your own children."

At that, the kittens burst out laughing and Father Cat rushed out to his vegetable garden with pink ears! Can you guess Father Cat's full name now?

Open House

Mamma Cat sighed and looked at her appointment book. "I don't know what we're going to do," she said. "We've been invited out by lots of cats recently, and we must ask them to visit us in return. But I just can't see how we're going to fit them all in."

Just then, Tiger Tail came tearing through the house like a whirlwind.

"I can't stop!" he called. "I've got to go and finish my project for the school Open Day."

That gave Mamma Cat an idea.

"We'll have an Open Day ourselves," she said. "We can invite everyone at the same time. We'll call it an Open House."

"Good idea," mumbled Father Cat, who was munching a sandwich. "You arrange it, dear. Invite whoever you like."

"I certainly will," said Mamma Cat, "but you are going to have to fix the hinges on the front door. It feels very wobbly every time I open it. We can't have it coming off in a visitor's paw."

"I'll do it tonight," said Father Cat. But, you know, with one thing and another, Father Cat never did get around to fixing the door....

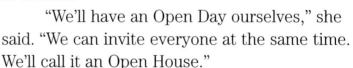

The day of the Open House was warm and sunny.
Mamma Cat prepared enormous amounts of delicious food.
The little cats helped put it on the table, only eating a tiny
bit on the way. Fluffy and Rolypoly gathered flowers to
decorate the living room and arranged them in every free
vase, bottle, and mug they could find. Honeybun and
Mopsy folded paper napkins into the most amazing
shapes. As for Tiger Tail, he was rushing here and
there, and no one was very sure *what* he was doing.

It was only when the guests began to arrive
that a guilty look came over Father Cat's face. He
remembered that he had not fixed the door. As
each visitor came in, he held his breath, but the
door, though wobbly, stayed firmly in place.
When the last cat had arrived, Father Cat
gave a sigh of relief.

But just then, Tiger Tail came tearing
in from outside. The door gave a wobble and
a wibble and made an *eeeeeeeeeah* sound.
Then it fell right off its hinges and out
onto the path.

There was a deafening silence.
Then Father Cat gave a little laugh.

"Well, it really is an Open House now!"
he chuckled.

The Honey Pot

One afternoon, Farmer Feather brought Mamma Cat a huge pot of honey. It was a pretty blue pot, filled to the brim with lovely golden honey from Farmer Feather's own bees.

"It's funny," he said. "My wife and I have had so much honey recently, we just don't seem to enjoy it anymore. I hope your hungry little ones will like this."

"I'm sure they will," said Mamma Cat. "Thank you very much, Farmer Feather."

When Tiger Tail saw the honey pot, he wanted to dip his little paw in right away.

"Just one little taste, Mamma!" he pleaded, but Mamma Cat was firm.

"I don't want sticky pawmarks all over the house," she said. "You can have some tomorrow, like everyone else."

That evening, Mamma Cat had no peace. Each little kitten in turn begged to be able to dip just one little paw into the honey. Even Father Cat was discovered lifting up the lid.

"No," said Mamma. "You will all have to wait until tomorrow."

Of course, that just made the rest of the family long to taste that honey even more. As she turned out the lights before bed that night, Mamma Cat herself couldn't resist taking a peek inside. And when she saw the golden honey, she dipped her paw just a little way into it. Mmmmm!

That night, one little kitten after another discovered that it was very hard to sleep without a taste of that honey. One by one, they crept into the kitchen and had just one – or maybe two – or maybe several more – tastes of the yummy sweet, sticky stuff. Even Father Cat slipped out of bed when the moon was high in the sky, and I'm sorry to say that he had *quite a few* tastes.

Next day, Mamma Cat saw sticky pawmarks on the kitchen door. She was pretty sure she knew what had happened, but she didn't feel she could scold anyone, as she had tasted the honey herself.

That evening at supper, Mamma announced, "Now you can all have as much honey as you like on your bread and butter."

"No thank you," said the little kittens. "We don't really feel like it today."

"What about you, dear?" asked Mamma Cat, turning to her husband.

"Not tonight, perhaps," he said.

Then Mamma lifted the lid of the honey pot with a smile.

"It's a good thing we all had a taste yesterday," she said, "because there isn't any left at *all* today!"

Five-Minute
Bedtime
Tales

Time For Bed!

There is a story for everyone with this enchanting
collection of sleepytime tales.

Contents

Fred-Under-the-Bed

When the children's mother saw that Jake and Rosie were still playing, she told them to go to bed at once.

"But there's a Fred under Jake's bed!" cried the twins.

"What *do* you mean?" asked their mother. "There's nothing under your beds except odd socks and probably more dust than there should be."

"But it's what happens to socks," said Jake. "They turn into sock monsters. Ours is called Fred."

"That's enough," said his mother. "Get into bed right now. I'm putting the light out, but I'll leave the door open."

Jake and Rosie jumped into bed, but by the light from the hall they could see right away that a funny little figure was crawling out from under Jake's bed. It was Fred. He seemed to be made of odd socks, including one of the ones with pompoms that Rosie had been given for Christmas.

"Has she gone?" he asked in a muffled voice. Sock monsters always talk like that.

"Yes, she has," whispered Rosie. "But if you're looking for socks again, you can't have any. We're fed up with finding only odd socks to wear."

"But I'm hungry," said the sock monster. "Isn't there anything else? I could manage a glove or a pair of mittens."

"We *need* those," said Jake. "We needed those socks, too."

"If I don't have something soon," said the sock monster, "I'm going to start munching your teddy bears."

"No!" cried Rosie. Now the twins knew that the sock monster was not a very nice monster, as monsters go.

"I know what to do!" whispered Jake. "You give him my scarf to nibble. I'll grab him!"

"Fnnnnffnnnfn!" shouted the sock monster, as Jake ran out of the room and down the stairs. There was no one about as he threw the sock monster into the washing machine and slammed the door.

Next morning, their mother put on a load of laundry. Later, when the twins saw it flapping on the line, they felt sure that the sock monster was gone for ever. Hmmm. What do you think?

The Magic Quilt

Once upon a time, there was a woman who loved to sew. She made beautiful dresses for her daughters and handsome suits for her sons. They were made of the richest, brightest fabrics she could afford. Long after the children had gone to bed, she would sit by the light of a single candle and sew into the night. In the morning, she would be up earlier than anyone else, ready to go out to work for her family.

But the years passed. One by one, her daughters got married and left home. Of course, their mother sewed every stitch of their wedding gowns. Her sons went off into the world to seek their fortunes. They settled in faraway lands. From time to time, they sent letters home to their mother, but in all her busy life, she had never learned to read. She kept the letters in a chest, tied up with ribbons, until a friend from the nearby town could come to tell her what they said.

As the woman grew older, she could no longer work. She still loved to sew, but she could not afford the costly fabrics she had used before. At last, she became too weak to look after herself. Her friend invited her to stay. All she took with her was the chest from the foot of her bed.

Too frail to walk, the old woman lay in bed each day, watching the patterns made by the sun as it moved around the walls.

"If only you could read," said her friend, "it would give you something to occupy your mind."

That night, the woman dreamed of a special book with pages of red and blue and gold, full of stories and memories. The book was magic. If you touched it, the book could carry you to countries far away. In her dream, the old woman flew around the world, visiting her sons and daughters and bouncing her grandchildren on her knee.

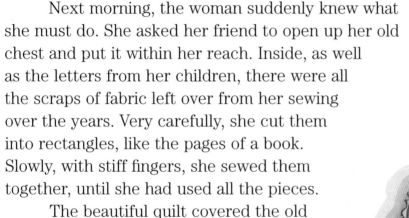

Next morning, the woman suddenly knew what she must do. She asked her friend to open up her old chest and put it within her reach. Inside, as well as the letters from her children, there were all the scraps of fabric left over from her sewing over the years. Very carefully, she cut them into rectangles, like the pages of a book. Slowly, with stiff fingers, she sewed them together, until she had used all the pieces.

The beautiful quilt covered the old woman's bed from top to toe. As she smoothed her fingers over the fabric, in her mind she journeyed to far off places, thinking of the memories held by each piece of fabric.

"This is a book that I *can* read," she said, and she never felt unhappy again.

A Bear With No Name

When a bear has found a good home, with children who love him, there is only one more thing he needs: a name. Having a name is what makes a bear feel he is no longer just one of hundreds of other bears, sitting on a toy shop shelf. A name gives a bear distinction. It helps him to know who he is. It is, in other words, Very Important.

And that is why, when the bear in this story had been in his new home for over a month and *still* hadn't been given a name, he began to feel very concerned.

"It's not difficult to think of a name," he muttered to himself. "I could be William, or Rufus, or Benjamin. Yes, Benjamin Bear is a good name. I don't know what's the matter with this family. You'd think they could have thought of something by now."

As a matter of fact, it wasn't very strange at all that the bear hadn't been given a name, for the little boy he now belonged to was only ten days old! The little boy could sleep, and he could cry, and he could drink his milk, but he couldn't do much else at all. He certainly couldn't *talk*. But the bear didn't understand about babies. He thought humans were like bears – able to walk and talk as soon as they were made.

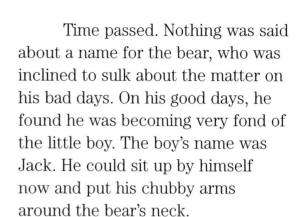

Time passed. Nothing was said about a name for the bear, who was inclined to sulk about the matter on his bad days. On his good days, he found he was becoming very fond of the little boy. The boy's name was Jack. He could sit up by himself now and put his chubby arms around the bear's neck.

"When he can talk," said the bear to himself, "Jack will give me a name. I know he will."

But things did not turn out as the bear expected. One morning, the little boy sat up in his bed and stretched out his arms. "Bear!" he said. "Bear! Bear!" It was his very first word.

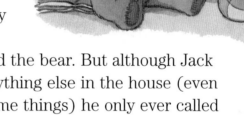

"It won't be long now," said the bear. But although Jack was soon finding words for everything else in the house (even making up his own words for some things) he only ever called the bear "Bear!"

Then, one day, Jack had a new baby sister. Her aunt gave her a bear of her own, and from the very beginning everyone called the new bear Honey.

"And what is your name?" Honey asked Jack's bear, when he introduced himself.

The bear mumbled, but he couldn't avoid answering.

"He calls me Bear," he said, waiting for Honey to laugh. But Honey didn't laugh.

"Oh, you are lucky," she said. "What a distinguished name. Only the very finest bear could possibly be called Bear!"

That night, when Jack snuggled down in his bed with his bear, he whispered, "Goodnight, Bear!" as he always did. And Bear could hardly sleep because he was almost bursting with pride.

"Goodnight, Boy!" he whispered back.

Oh No, Not Again!

There was once a little elf who lived in a tree trunk. His mother and his granny lived there too. The elf's name was Juniper Jingle, and everyone liked him.

But Juniper's mother and granny found him very hard to live with. The daytimes were fine. It was nighttime when the problems started. You see, Juniper had wonderful dreams. Every night he dreamed he was flying over the mountains, or riding a unicorn, or dancing among the stars. They were lovely, magical dreams but they always had the same result. Juniper tossed and turned so much in his sleep that he fell out of bed.

You may not think that falling out of bed is such a bad thing, especially if there are soft cushions on the floor. But then you probably don't live in a tree. When Juniper fell with a thud, the whole tree shook. Mrs Jingle woke up. Old Mrs Jingle woke up. The squirrel who lived in the branches woke up. The rabbits who lived in the roots woke up (and there were a lot of them!) And the little bird who was building a nest at the very top of the tree had to start all over again. No one was happy except Juniper Jingle, who slept on as if nothing had happened … on the floor.

Mrs Jingle had tried everything to keep Juniper in his bed. She put up rails … but he climbed them in his sleep. She tucked him in tight … but he threw off his covers without waking up. It was hopeless. Finally, she decided she must go to see the Fidget Fairy for a magic spell.

The Fidget Fairy was outspoken and not very polite. "It's his bed that's the problem," she said firmly.

"I can assure you it's the finest, most comfortable bed in the whole wood," protested Mrs Jingle.

"But it's a bed for an ordinary elf," said the fairy, "and Juniper is a most extraordinary elf. An imagination like that should be encouraged. I will give you a spell to make him an imaginary bed, and everything will be well."

Mrs Jingle was not convinced, but when she got home she said the spell exactly as she had been taught it. Juniper's old bed disappeared … and nothing came in its place. Mrs Jingle was just about to go back to the fairy to complain when Juniper walked in.

"Wow!" he said. "Wow and double wow! That's a *wonderful* bed!" And he climbed up into mid-air and lay there, as comfortable as could be.

Juniper still has wonderful dreams, but no matter how much he tosses and turns, he never hits the floor. Mrs Jingle is happy. Old Mrs Jingle is happy. The squirrel and the rabbits are happy. And the little bird at the top of the tree now has the finest nest in the wood filled with babies of her own.

Aunt Aggie Comes to Stay

The very first time Aunt Aggie came to stay with Louisa and her family, no one was prepared. They didn't guess that Aunt Aggie would arrive in a *truck*, or that she would bring *so much* with her! This is what she brought:

a huge trunk with exciting labels on it...

one pink, one orange, one yellow, one blue, and one brown case...

a picnic hamper that was extraordinarily heavy...

a guitar in a case with flowers painted all over it...

a striped bicycle with little flags on the handlebars...

several large bags with very strange things peeking out...

a parrot in a cage...

and...

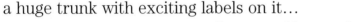

the biggest bunch of flowers you have *ever* seen!

By the time Aunt Aggie had moved everything in, Louisa's house felt very full. But Louisa didn't mind at all – there were such interesting things to see. Aunt Aggie seemed to have been *everywhere*, and she had wonderful stories to tell. Louisa *loved* having her to stay.

At last the day came when it was time for Aunt Aggie to go home. Into the truck went a huge trunk, one pink, one orange, one yellow, one blue, and one brown case, a picnic hamper, a guitar in a case, a striped bicycle, several large bags, a parrot in a cage, a huge box that had once contained a dishwasher, and Aunt Aggie.

"Goodbye!" she called, as she reversed dangerously into the road. "See you next year!"

It wasn't until ten minutes later that someone said, "Where's Louisa?" and someone else said, "*What* was in that dishwasher box?"

An anxious five minutes passed, and Aunt Aggie's truck came squealing up to the door.

"I can see," laughed Aunt Aggie, "you've been thinking what I've been thinking!"

That evening, when Louisa was safely tucked up in bed, and Aunt Aggie was far away, the little girl said, "Will she come back next year?"

"I'm afraid so," said Louisa's dad.

"Of course she will," said Louisa's mother.

"And will it be just the same?" asked Louisa.

"Yes," said Louisa's dad, "except we'll be checking *everything* in the truck before she drives away."

"Oh," said Louisa, and she fell fast asleep. After all, she thought, she had a whole year to think of a new plan.

The Babyish Bear

When Jack was given a big present for his birthday, he was impressed. It was from Mrs Marino, an elderly lady who lived nearby. Jack had never paid much attention to her before. He thought she was slightly strange, because she wore funny clothes and talked to herself as she walked down the street. But a present was a present, so maybe old Mrs Marino had hidden depths.

As soon as he had ripped off the paper, Jack changed his mind. It was a bear! A great big fluffy teddy bear with a ribbon around his neck. Even Jack's mother hid a smile.

"How lovely, sweetheart," she said. "You must say thank you to Mrs Marino when you see her."

Jack's mind was already on other problems. The bear had to be hidden – and fast. His friends were coming to his party in a couple of hours, and there was no way they could see this bear. If only it wasn't so enormous…

He tried to hide it in cupboards.
He tried to push it under the bed.
He tried to stuff it into the bag where the dirty laundry was kept.

Nothing worked. The bear was *there*. It was too big to hide.

Jack tried placing it in various positions around the house. Maybe it could just blend with the furniture somewhere? But he found that whenever he went back into the room, kind of pretending he didn't know there was a bear in there, the first thing to catch his eye was that silly, fluffy face!

It was almost time for the party when Jack had a brilliant idea.

"If I hurry, I've just got time to go and thank Mrs Marino," he told his mother. She was suspicious, of course, but she let him go.

Jack struggled down the street with the bear. When Mrs Marino opened the door, his words came out in a rush. "Mrs-Marino-thank-you-very-much-for-my-present-but-it's-my-party-and-I'm-afraid-he-might-get-damaged-so-could-you-keep-him-for-me-this-afternoon-please?"

Mrs Marino looked puzzled. "Well, you won't want a bear at your age, will you? Did you like the watch?"

Jack shook his head. What watch?

Then Mrs Marino showed him the little opening in the bear's back where you could tuck things away. And she gave him the amazing watch that was inside and explained that she thought the bear would stop it getting squashed or stood on among all his presents.

"I was right," Jack told his mother when he got home. "She *is* strange, but she's okay too. More than okay. Oh look, it's *time* for my party!"

Rainbow Ribbons

When an elf goes courting, he always takes the lady of his choice some ribbons for her hair. Elf girls are proud of their hair, which is thick and shiny. It also helps to hide their ears, which, as you know, are large and pointed. (Now there is nothing wrong with large, pointed ears, but some elf girls have been taking too much notice of the fairies, whose ears are so tiny you can hardly see them.)

Elderflower Elf went shopping one day for ribbons to take to Emmeline. He stood for some time in the shop full of ribbons and laces of every kind. It was hard to decide which ribbons to buy. In the end, he chose green ones, to match dear Emmeline's eyes. Then he wandered home in a haze of happiness, thinking about meeting her later, and fell into a ditch as a result, annoying a frog who lived there.

Unfortunately, Emmeline's beautiful eyes lit up for only a moment when she saw the ribbons.

"I was hoping you would bring orange ones," Emmeline sighed. "Elderflower? Elderflower?"

But the young elf was already gone, running back to the shop as fast as he could. Naturally, he didn't look where he was going, so he had another close encounter with the frog who lived in the ditch.

Emmeline considered the new orange ribbons for a second – before expressing a preference for blue.

Back went Elderflower. *Splash!* You guessed it. The frog was *not* happy. He wasn't happy ten minutes later, either, when Elderflower dashed by with red ribbons and landed right on his nose.

Back at her rose bower, Emmeline saw Elderflower approaching once more, clutching bunches of red ribbons. She sighed. Somehow there was something about Elderflower that just didn't appeal to her, especially when he was panting so hard he couldn't talk. She was just about to send him off for violet ribbons, just to get rid of him, when…

"I wonder if these are to your taste, my dear?" said a deep voice, and a jumping gentleman in green offered her a bow of beautiful rainbow ribbons.

Well, Emmeline married her frog and lived happily ever after. And Elderflower? He realized how well ribbons sell and is doing very well for himself in his own little shop in an oak tree!

213

A Puppet For Polly

For her fourth birthday, Polly asked for a puppet. She didn't ask nicely. She didn't say "please". She said, "I want a puppet!" very, very loudly. That was the kind of little girl Polly Chin was.

Polly's dad was firm. She couldn't have everything she wanted, he said. But Polly's Aunt Naomi just smiled. On the little girl's birthday morning, there was a package from Aunt Naomi and inside was a big, beautiful, clown puppet. Polly ignored all her other presents and started playing with it at once.

She found she could make the puppet do anything she liked, and she loved it.

"Time for swimming!" called her dad a little later. "Get your things, sweetheart."

"No!" said Polly. "Come with me, Mr Clown. We'll hide in my bedroom."

"No!" said the puppet.

Polly was so surprised, she dropped him!

"Ow!" cried Mr Clown. "I wish I hadn't come here, if that's how I'm going to be treated."

"I'm sorry," said the little girl, which was not something she often said. She picked up Mr Clown and carried him to her room. She was going to hide under the bed and play with him

214

when her dad had given up trying to make her come out, but somehow she didn't like the knowing look the puppet was giving her… Polly collected her swimming things and left.

That night, after swimming, and a special lunch, and her birthday party, and lots more presents, Polly played with her puppet again. But Dad was already calling up the stairs.

"Time for bed, birthday girl!"

"Not yet!" shouted Polly.

"No way!" said the puppet. Once again, Polly looked in disbelief.

"I mean," Mr Clown went on, "we haven't finished playing yet, and I won't be sleepy for hours. That man is rude and mean."

Now those were the kinds of things that I'm afraid Polly had very often said to her father, but she felt angry to hear someone else saying them.

"He's *not* rude and mean!" she said. "And I'm ready for bed. In you go!" She pushed the puppet into her toybox and shut the lid.

"Quite right," said Mr Clown, much to Polly's surprise.

It didn't take Polly long to realize that when *she* was naughty, *Mr Clown* was naughty too. And when she was good… well, you can imagine. Her dad noticed the difference.

"You know," he told his older sister Naomi, "ever since she's had that clown, she's been a nicer child. What a relief!"

Naomi smiled. "I remember" she said, "how it worked with a naughty little boy *I* grew up with."

But Polly's dad, like Polly sometimes, pretended not to hear.

Why Am I Blue?

Once upon a time, there was a little blue elephant. Little Blue lived with his family on a dusty plain, munching and marching, marching and munching. When he wasn't munching *or* marching, what he loved best was rolling in the mud of a waterhole.

One day, the elephants came to a waterhole that was not as muddy as usual. It had clear, clean water, sparkling in the sunshine.

"No unseemly haste, please!" said Great-Grandmother Elephant, who could see that some of the younger members of her family were about to break into a trot. They swayed their trunks to show that they understood and moved forward at a sedate pace toward the pool. Mother Elephant ushered Little Blue to the front. She didn't want him to be left behind.

Little Blue reached the waterhole and looked down. Another little elephant looked back at him.

216

It was the first time that Little Blue had seen his reflection. It was wonderful! He swung his trunk one way. So did the other elephant. He swung it the other way. The other elephant did the same. Then he delicately put his trunk into the water and kissed his reflection.

It was only when he was full of the clear, clean water that the little elephant turned to his mother and asked, "Why am I blue?" Little Blue could see now that none of the other elephants looked at all like him.

"You are blue because blue is right for *you*," Little Blue's mother replied. "Some elephants are pink, some are blue, some are yellow, and some are like me, sort of dusty."

But Little Blue wasn't sure. He had never seen another blue elephant. He felt strange and different.

Then, one day, far away across the plain, he saw a wonderful sight. Pink, yellow and, yes, *blue* elephants were strolling along just ahead. Without a second thought, Little Blue scampered to meet them.

The new elephants were very friendly. Little Blue felt so happy to see other grown-up elephants who looked just like him. "I shall stay with these elephants," he said.

But that night, as he tried to sleep under the stars, Little Blue realized he didn't really belong with the strange elephants. His own mother was sleeping faraway across the plain, and maybe she was missing her blue baby. All by himself, under the huge moon, he trotted back to his own family.

"I'm so glad you're back, Little Blue," whispered his mother, sleepily.

"Mother, I like being blue," he whispered back. "Blue is just right."

"And you are just right, too," said his mother. "Now go to sleep, Little Blue. *All* elephants need their rest, even blue ones."

Are You There, Mr Bear?

All day long, strange noises came from Mr Bear's house. There was clattering and banging and, I'm sorry to say, some angry words, too. It went on for hours, and everyone wondered what Mr Bear could possibly be doing. It sounded as though he was moving furniture around, but no one was brave enough to knock on the door to find out. Mr Bear had always been short tempered. Just recently, he had been more sharp and snappy than usual.

"Maybe he's spring cleaning," said Ragged Rabbit.

"Don't be ridiculous," replied his wife. "It's August."

By the end of the afternoon, a small crowd had gathered outside Mr Bear's house. Still the strange noises went on.

"He wouldn't hear even if we did knock and offer to help," said a panda, which made everyone feel much better.

As the moon rose in the sky, the animals wandered back to their own homes. Gradually the noises from Mr Bear's house stopped. There was complete silence for half an hour. Then the gentle sound of Mr Bear's snoring could be heard, like a big cat purring.

The next morning, Ragged Rabbit happened to be passing just as Mr Bear came out of his front door.

"Morning, Rabbit!" he beamed. "And a wonderful morning it is, too!"

"M-m-m-morning," stammered Ragged Rabbit. It was a very long time since he had heard Mr Bear say anything cheerful. He watched in amazement as Mr Bear strolled off down the street, greeting everyone he met with a friendly word and a wave.

When Ragged Rabbit told his wife about it at lunchtime, she put down her spoon at once. "It's not natural," she said, "and I'm going to find out what's happened. I'm going to see Mr Bear."

Much to her husband's surprise, she was back in five minutes.

"I met Mr Bear in the lane," she said, "and soon found out all about it. He's been bad tempered because he hasn't been getting a wink of sleep.

Some birds built their nest under the eaves and kept him awake with their twittering. All day yesterday he was hauling his big brass bed downstairs, where he can sleep in peace. He was cheerful because he'd just had his first full night's sleep in weeks."

"So it's safe to visit him again?" asked Ragged Rabbit.

"Not for long," replied Mrs Rabbit darkly. "A family of mice has just moved in under the sitting room floorboards. Their scampering is worse than twittering any day."

All at Sea

Petunia Panda was reading a bedtime book to her little ones. It was a rhyme about an owl and a pussy-cat who sailed away in a beautiful pea-green boat. All the baby pandas loved it, especially Patrick. His mind was so full of sailing and bong-trees and piggywigs that he began to dream about them as soon as his head touched the pillow. But Patrick's dream started to go wrong from the very beginning.

Patrick's boat wasn't pea-green. It was red. And he wasn't sailing away with a pussy-cat sitting quietly in the boat. Oh no. He was sailing with a kangaroo!

"Please don't bounce!" cried Patrick. "Please don't bounce!"

"Of course not," said the kangaroo. But kangaroos are so used to bouncing, they don't always know when they are doing it. The kangaroo in Patrick's red boat was good for a very long time … until Patrick saw an island on the horizon.

"Look!" he shouted.

"Where?" cried the kangaroo. And she bounced in excitement.

The next moment, Patrick found himself in the wettest water he had ever known. It was much wetter than water in a bathtub, and it was moving about! As the waves splashed into his ears, Patrick looked around for the kangaroo.

"Come up here!" she called. The upturned boat was floating nearby, and the clever kangaroo was sitting right on top of it. She dragged Patrick out of the water so that he could dry in the warm sun.

Slowly the upturned boat drifted toward the island. Patrick held on tight to the kangaroo, who had an extraordinarily good sense of balance. (It must have been all that bouncing.)

At last the boat landed with a bump on the sandy shore of the island. Patrick wondered what would happen next.

"I think we're meant to dance by the light of the moon," said the kangaroo, almost as if she had read Patrick's thoughts.

"But it's daytime," said Patrick, looking up at the palm trees. And just as he did so, a coconut tumbled down and bounced off his head.

"Ouch!" To Patrick's amazement, he wasn't asleep any longer, but his little brother Peter was banging him on the head with his toy kangaroo.

"I've been awake for ages," announced Peter. "I'm glad you've woken up at last."

"So am I," said Patrick, rubbing his head. "So am I."

The Rainy Day

Mrs Millie Mouse looked out of the window at the rain "Poor, poor Daphne!" she sighed. "Today of all days!"

Mr Mouse knew exactly what she meant, but he was busy reading his newspaper and didn't want to be drawn into a conversation about The Wedding. He had heard about nothing else for months. Mrs Mouse's sister Daphne was getting married. She was not a young mouse, but running her gardening business had left her little time for going to the dinners and parties where most mice meet their partners. Then, one day, she had visited a busy carpenter mouse to order a fence. The rest was history.

Mrs Mouse put on her raincoat and hat and hurried out into the rain. She needed to visit her friends to discuss the dreadful calamity. They had to decide what to do with the mountains of food they had all been preparing. More important still, what were they to do with the extraordinary and amazingly huge hats they had all made, each trying to outdo the other?

Mrs Mouse found all her friends at Mrs Martha Mouse's house, which was the biggest in the wood.

"I'd love to offer to have the wedding here," cried Mrs Martha Mouse, "but there simply isn't room for three hundred guests. I wish we could postpone the wedding, but what about all the food? My cook has been working hard all week!"

"Underground, maybe?" queried Millie Mouse. But one of the others cried out at once.

"Oh no! It would be so dark and cramped. And my hat won't fit any of the passages!"

"Besides," said Martha Mouse, "I refuse to have anything to do with those rabbits after what happened to my rock garden." (Martha Mouse's rock garden had become a large hole overnight, when a young rabbit with little sense of direction decided to pop up and look at the moon.)

Now you may notice that we have not yet met Daphne and her fiancé Tom. As a matter of fact, neither of them wanted all this fuss, which had been arranged entirely by the mouse ladies without stopping to ask if it was wanted at all.

While the ladies chattered, and the rain poured down, the two mice who should have been more worried than anyone were smiling happily. Their dream of a quiet wedding had come true after all as they stood beneath a young oak tree with only the Reverend Alfred Mouse for company.

"I love the rain," whispered Daphne, "don't you?"

"Almost as much," whispered Tom, "as I love you."

Trouble in the Toy Box

When Leila went to bed at the end of a long and exciting day, she fell asleep almost at once. It was her birthday. In the morning, there had been presents and a special breakfast. Then her dad had taken her to the swimming pool and she had whizzed down the water chute seven times, which was more than she had ever whizzed before. After lunch, Leila's friends came to her party, and there were more presents. Just after the friends went home, Leila's granny visited and there were even more presents. And that is why the trouble began.

While Leila slept peacefully in her bed, there was a terrible groaning and sighing from her toy box. It was a special box, shaped like a pirate's chest, that her uncle had given her *last* year for her birthday.

"That panda is sitting on my elbow!" said a grumpy voice.

"You'd feel worse if you had a train standing on your toes," moaned another voice.

"That's no fun," cried the train. "I hate it when my wheels are wiggly."

"We were fine in here," said the ragdoll firmly, "until all these new toys arrived today. They should go."

"Did you see how happy Leila was when she opened us?" asked a yo-yo. "If anyone has to go, it's the old toys."

"I can't stand this any more," said the old panda, who was very worn and fragile. "I've got to get out of here!" He pushed and wriggled until he could open the lid of the chest and tumble out onto the floor. Lots of the other toys followed him, and the train, who was sometimes pretty clumsy, knocked the lid shut as he jumped out.

"Now we're stuck," said the ragdoll.

"I don't care," the panda replied. "It's better out here."

Next morning, Leila's dad shook his head when he saw all the toys over the floor, but he soon realized it would be hard to squeeze them all back into the toy box.

Just then, Leila's uncle arrived. "I'm sorry I couldn't make it yesterday," he said, "but I've brought your present today."

"Oh no!" Leila's dad groaned. "We've got enough trouble finding room for the presents we've got already."

But Leila's uncle just grinned. "Then it's a good thing I couldn't think of a different present this year," he said. And he carried in … another enormous toy box!

That night there was no grumbling and groaning among the toys. They slept just as quietly as Leila.

What's That?

One night, Baby Bear woke up to find the moon shining right through the window onto his bed. Suddenly, Baby Bear felt wide awake. And what's more, he felt hungry! He rubbed his tummy and tried to think sleepy thoughts, but it was no good. He knew that downstairs in the kitchen there was some apple pie. His tummy *needed* that pie. Pushing back his quilt, Baby Bear scrambled out of bed.

In his bedroom, the moonlight made it easy to see where he was going. But outside in the hallway, it was very dark. Baby Bear peered through the blackness. Putting the light on might wake Mamma Bear, who was, as Baby Bear knew only too well, an extraordinarily light sleeper. In any case, he was too small to reach the light switch.

Baby Bear set off along the carpet, feeling in front of him with his paws at every step. When he couldn't feel anything at all in front of him, he knew he had reached the stairs. Although it was still just as dark, at least he could hold onto the stair rail now.

"Not far to that pie now," said Baby Bear to himself. But just then, he heard a noise.

226

"What's that?" he worried.

There was silence. After a few moments, Baby Bear went on down to the bottom of the stairs.

But as he turned toward the kitchen, he heard another sound.

"What's that?" he wondered.

There was silence again. Cautiously, Baby Bear put his hand on the kitchen doorknob. He opened the door rapidly to get the squeaking over as quickly as possible and…

"What's that?" cried a deep voice.

"What's that?" squeaked Baby Bear.

As the kitchen light was flipped on, he found himself face to tummy with Papa Bear … and Papa Bear was holding a large slice of apple pie!

The two bears looked at each other for a long minute.

"If I gave you a little bit of pie," said Papa Bear, "you won't need to wake Mamma Bear, will you?"

"If I don't wake Mamma Bear," said Baby Bear, "you won't wake Mamma Bear, will you?"

"It's a deal," said Papa Bear. "We must munch very quietly."

And so they did.

Birthday Books

Grown-up people can be very bad at remembering things. They forget keys and hats and anniversaries almost every day. So how is it they (usually) remember your birthday? That's the work of the birthday fairy, who whispers in their ears a week or so before each important day.

The fairies have a special book, where all the birthdays in the world are written down (even grown-up ones). Long, long ago, there was just one Birthday Book. Nowadays, there are hundreds and hundreds of them, all kept in the Lilac Library. A very old elf has been the librarian for years and years. He is helped by a team of lively little elves, who are very good at running up and down the ladders that reach up to the highest shelves.

One day, there was a terrible commotion in the Lilac Library. A book had gone missing! It was the one for October 17th, Volume 96.

"It must have been misplaced," said the Chief Librarian, when an anxious fairy reported the problem. "Elves! Go and search every shelf to find the missing volume!"

The elves searched all day. Then they lit little lamps and searched all night. But they could not find the missing book.

The fairy concerned was beside herself with anxiety. "I must start reminding parents today," she said. "It's already the 10th of October."

"Don't worry, my dear," cried the Chief Librarian. "This has never happened before and it won't happen now, if I have anything to do with it. Come back in half an hour and I'll have a list of names for you."

As soon as the fairy had gone, the old elf pressed a secret button under his desk. A whole shelf of books swung open, and the Chief Librarian slipped inside to his secret room. It wasn't full of spells and potions. It wasn't full of cobwebs and cauldrons. It had a neat little desk and a computer with a big smile on its screen.

"Can I help you, Librarian?" it asked.

The old elf's fingers flew over the keyboard. In no time at all, the computer whirred and whizzed. The printer clicked and hummed. And a long list of all the birthdays for October 17th curled out of the machine.

When the Chief Librarian emerged from his room, the fairy was delighted with the list, although the elf swore her to secrecy about his back-up system. "It doesn't go with the elf image somehow," he explained.

And when the Chief Librarian got back to his desk, he found he had been sitting on the missing volume all the time. (You see, elves are often a lot like grown-ups, too.)

229

The Tumbling Clown

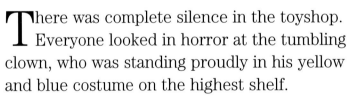

T here was complete silence in the toyshop. Everyone looked in horror at the tumbling clown, who was standing proudly in his yellow and blue costume on the highest shelf.

"Don't be ridiculous!" cried the fluffy panda. "All your stuffing will fall out!"

"I can't bear to look!" whispered the little blue rabbit.

"If you're silly enough to do it, I can't stop you," said the jumping frog. "But even I wouldn't attempt a leap like that."

The tumbling clown put his nose in the air. "None of you has any idea of my abilities," he said grandly. "I was made to tumble and tumble I will! Can I have a long drumroll, please, Pink Teddy Bear?"

"Don't do it, Teddy!" yelled the panda, but that bear's only real skill was playing the drum and he went right ahead.

Drrr! Drrr! Drrr! Drrr!
The tumbling clown raised
his hands in the air.

He jumped off the shelf…
making a perfect somersault…

and a double back flip…
He touched his toes…

and landed on his feet on the back
of one of the elephants belonging
to the toy Noah's ark.

"There'll be no stopping him now,"
muttered the panda.

"Is it over?" asked the little blue rabbit.

"Wow! That was great!" cried the jumping
frog. "Will you show me how you did it?"

"Of course," said the tumbling clown.

So the next day, the jumping frog
performed an even more amazing acrobatic
display than usual. The day after that (much to
his own surprise) the panda tried a small
somersault himself. And by the end of the week,
even the little blue rabbit could do a double-eared
spin with tail twist.

So, if you have a little brother or sister
whose toys are always flying out of the bed or
buggy, you'll know it's not the baby's fault at all.
Those toys have been taught by the tumbling
clown, and they won't stay still no matter what
you do!

A Bear at Bathtime

Johanna wanted to take her bear everywhere. She took him to playgroup. She took him to visit her friends. She took him to the park. And, of course, she took him to bed with her. The only problem with Johanna and her bear was bathtime. Every night there was a battle.

"Sweetheart, he *can't* go in the bathtub," Johanna's mother would say. "He'll get soaking and soggy. You won't be able to take him to bed with you and I'm pretty sure his paws would shrink."

But Johanna didn't want to listen. She was sure that her bear was just as alive as any of her friends. He listened to everything she said. And her friends didn't get soggy in the bathtub! Johanna looked carefully at her hands and feet. They certainly didn't shrink in the water. Johanna decided her mother was wrong.

But mothers can be very determined. Each night at bathtime there were loud words from Johanna, and there were firm words from her mother. There was not very much at all from her teddy bear, who was forced to sit on a shelf until Johanna was dry and ready for bed.

232

I suppose it had to happen one day… Johanna's Aunt May came to babysit one evening. Aunt May knew, of course, that bears don't go in bathtubs, but she didn't know she had to watch Johanna every *second* of bathtime. In went the bear, hidden by the bubbles. It wasn't until Johanna dragged the soaking, furry toy out of the bathtub that Aunt May saw what happened. She was horrified.

"You can't take a wet bear to bed with you, and that's final," she told the little girl. Well, there were loud words from Johanna, and there were firm words from her aunt. There was plenty of dripping from the teddy bear.

Aunts can be very determined, too. When Johanna went to sleep at last, Aunt May took the bear down to the drier and popped him in. Much later, she tucked him into bed beside Johanna.

Next morning, Johanna's mother looked curiously at Johanna and her bear as they sat down for breakfast.

"Your bear looks smaller," she said with a frown.

Secretly, Johanna thought so, too. But she couldn't say that to her mother. Johannas can be determined, too.

"He isn't smaller," she said. "It's just that *I've* grown."

No More Cake!

When Agatha Mouse hopped on the scales in the bathroom one morning, she let out a little shriek of alarm. All the little mice, who were cleaning their teeth after breakfast, jumped.

"Oh no," groaned Ethel. "It's no-more-cake-time."

"It certainly is," sighed their mother. "I'm afraid it's no-more-cake-for-a-long-time."

The little mice sighed, too. They knew what their mother was like during no-more-cake times. She was miserable. She was grumpy. She had to shut her eyes when they walked past all the bakeries in town (and often bumped into other mice as a result). But worst of all, she stopped baking. She didn't make pies. She didn't make cookies. She didn't make puddings. And, of course, she didn't make cakes! Agatha Mouse was well known as the *best* cook in the area. When she stopped baking, it wasn't just a blow to the little mice. They found that several of their friends stopped calling, and interest in their school lunchboxes suddenly disappeared.

But there was no stopping Agatha when she made up her mind. She decided she needed more exercise, too, so she walked to school to collect the little mice instead of zooming along in her little red car. The little ones didn't mind having to walk home, but it made them late for the latest episode of *The Masked Mouse* on television each day. As they trooped home, no one would have guessed that they really were a very happy mouse family.

Agatha Mouse's no-more-cake times could sometimes last for weeks. The little mice gritted their teeth and tried not to think about muffins and pies. You can imagine how surprised they were when, only a couple of days later, they came home from a game of hide-the-acorn to find Mrs Mouse baking and singing in the kitchen.

"So it's not no-more-cake-time any more?" asked Ethel.

"No," smiled Agatha. "It's no-more-being-naughty-little-mice-time. It's finding-your-mother's-slippers-for-her-time. It's can-we-do-anything-to-help-you-dear-mother-time."

The little mice looked at each other. What *was* she talking about?

Agatha Mouse gave them all a big hug and an acorn muffin.

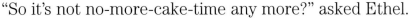

"My dears," she said, "you are big little mice now, and that's how you must behave. We're going to have some babies! That's why the scales said I was heavier. Now get ready for bed. And make the most of it! Very soon it's going to be waking-up-in-the-middle-of-the-night-time!"

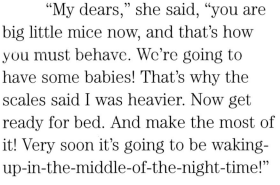

The Sniffles

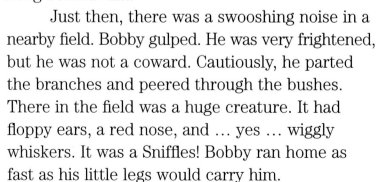

B obby Bunny was getting ready to go out to play when his mother called him back.

"You need your scarf on a day like this," she said. "We don't want you catching the sniffles, do we?"

Bobby was puzzled. "How do Sniffles look?" he asked.

"Droopy ears, a red nose, and wiggly whiskers," said his father from behind his newspaper.

Bobby ran out to join his friends. He had a wonderful time. When at last he realized he must hurry home, the sun was already beginning to go down.

The trees made dark shadows on the lane as Bobby scuttled along. It grew darker. Bobby was a brave little bunny, but he suddenly began to think about the Sniffles. More than once he turned his head to make sure there wasn't a Sniffles creeping along behind him.

Just then, there was a swooshing noise in a nearby field. Bobby gulped. He was very frightened, but he was not a coward. Cautiously, he parted the branches and peered through the bushes. There in the field was a huge creature. It had floppy ears, a red nose, and … yes … wiggly whiskers. It was a Sniffles! Bobby ran home as fast as his little legs would carry him.

"Bobby!" cried his mother. "We're so glad you're home.
But whatever is the matter?"

"It's the Sniffles!" cried Bobby. "I saw it in a field.
It had floppy ears and a red shiny nose. And its
whiskers were wiggly."

Father Bunny looked puzzled for a moment.
Then he grinned. "That sounds like the Sniffles.
all right," he said. "Let's go and see if we can
find it, son. We can't have a Sniffles
around here."

So Bobby Bunny and his father
walked quietly down the lane. When
they reached the right place, Bobby
pulled at his father's coat and pointed.

Very carefully, Father
Bunny parted the bushes.
Then he shone his
powerful flashlight
right onto the face of …
a scarecrow!

Suddenly, Bobby
felt a whole lot better.

On the way home, his father explained what the sniffles really were.
"I've learned something very important tonight," announced Bobby
with a smile. "It's not catching the sniffles you have to worry about, it's the
sniffles catching *you*!"

The Balloon Bear

When a cross little girl called Emily went to the fair with her grandma, she was very hard to please. Grandma bravely went on all the rides, but Emily said they were boring. Grandma bought Emily sweets and treats, but the little girl still didn't smile. Then Emily spotted a man selling balloons of every size and shape. "I want one of those," she said.

Grandma was tired and wanted her granddaughter to be happy, so she let Emily choose a balloon shaped like a bear. Emily didn't say thank you when the string was put into her hand. She just marched off toward the gates and home, with Grandma behind her.

Maybe it was because Emily was in such a hurry that a lady coming the other way bumped into her. It was only a little bump, but Emily let go of her balloon. The bear went floating up into the air and was out of reach before Emily even noticed it was gone.

"Buy me another one!" demanded the little girl. Grandma looked for the balloon man, but he had disappeared.

"I want to go home," said Emily. "I've had a horrible time."

Grandma was a very patient woman, but she was beginning to feel almost as cross as Emily.

What Emily and her grandma didn't notice as they walked home was that the balloon bear was bobbing along above them. He was still there when they reached Emily's gate and saw her mother cutting flowers.

"How was the fair?" she asked.

"Boring," said Emily.

"And the rides?"

"Boring."

"You must have had a very boring afternoon," said Emily's mother to her grandma with a sympathetic smile. At that moment, the balloon bear floated gently down, down, down, onto the roses. *POP!* it went – just behind Emily, who sat down with a bump and a surprised expression on her face.

"Well, there *was* one bit I did enjoy," said Grandma with a grin.

And all three, including Emily, laughed together at last.

One by One

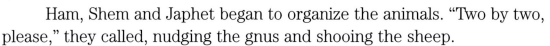

Mr Noah studied his charts. "I've built it exactly as I was told," he said to his wife, "but still, it doesn't look right somehow."

"The ark is fine," said Mrs Noah. "It's just the door that looks out of proportion. Are you sure you got the measurements right?"

"I've checked and checked," replied her husband. "It's high time we started loading the animals. I don't like the look of those clouds."

Ham, Shem and Japhet began to organize the animals. "Two by two, please," they called, nudging the gnus and shooing the sheep.

Dutifully, the animals lined up. And although there was a little pushing and shoving from the hippos, and the jaguars were taking a suspiciously friendly interest in the rabbits in front of them, it was all pretty orderly.

"Let the loading begin!" cried Mr Noah grandly. Two by two, up the plank, trotted the flamingos and the porcupines. Two by two came the butterflies and the peacocks. Two by two came those difficult hippos…

Ooops! Oh dear! There was no doubt about it, two hippos side by side would *not* fit through the door.

"I knew it!" cried Mr Noah. "I'm afraid you'll just have to go in one by one. It doesn't sound quite right, I know, but as long as two of every creature are on board, it can't really matter."

One by one went the zebras. One by one went the rhinos and the kangaroos. One by one went the elephants… Ooops! Oh dear! There just was no way that even one elephant would fit through the door.

"That settles it!" said Mr Noah. "Those elephants are meant to be on board. Although I'm sure I've done everything I was told, I simply must have made a mistake. Come on, Ham, we've got work to do!" Mr Noah set to work there and then to make a much larger doorway with two fine doors.

After that, there was no trouble loading the animals, and as the clouds gathered overhead, Mr Noah consulted his lists for the last time.

"I'm missing one tiny flea!" he called. "Mrs Flea, come along please!"

As he spoke, a tiny speck hopped off his chart and jumped into the ark.

Mr Noah peered at the paper. "Bless my soul, what a difference a zero makes," he said. "No wonder I got the measurements wrong. Now let's hope there's room on that ark for *me*!"

Clip, Clip, Clop

Dusty the horse leaned over the gate. "What are you doing, Percy?" he asked.

"Ssssh!" said Percy Pig. "Don't interrupt me, old friend. I'm reading my book."

Dusty blew through his nose rudely. "Poo!" he snorted. "I don't know why you want to do that. Come and play Chase with me instead."

"You don't like reading because you're not very good at it, Dusty," said Percy. "And that's because you don't do it enough. You need some practice, that's all. Then you could read just as well as I can – and you'd like it a lot more."

Dusty kicked up his heels and snorted again. "It still seems boring to me," he said, "and books are always about silly things anyway."

"Well, that's where you're wrong, old friend," replied Percy. "This book happens to be about a horse, and it's very interesting."

Dusty looked dubious. He tried to peer over Percy's shoulder, but Percy turned away.

"I really can't read with you blowing in my ear," he complained. "Let me finish this story and then I'll come for a trot down the road with you."

Dusty was not in a very good mood by the time Percy joined him. He was sulking and sighing as the two of them set off. In fact, he deliberately trotted off at a faster pace than Percy's little legs could go.

"Just a minute, Dusty," puffed Percy, "there's something I need to talk to you about."

"Well?" said Dusty shortly.

"It's just that in my book," said Percy, ignoring the snort this brought from his friend, "the horse went *clip, clop, clip, clop* down the lane. But I couldn't help noticing that you're going *clip, clip, clop, clop, clip, clip, clop, clop*."

Dusty looked down at his hooves. One of his shoes was very loose and he'd been sulking too much to notice.

A quick trip to the blacksmith soon fixed Dusty's problem. "It's a good thing you got it fixed so quickly," said the blacksmith. "You could have hurt yourself."

Nowadays, Dusty has a new respect for books. So if you happen to see a horse and a pig reading together in a field, you'll know who they are, won't you?

Be Brave, Lian!

Lian was afraid of dragons. Although everyone told her not to be silly, she lived in a country where the storybooks were *full* of dragons. It was true that no one had seen one for years, but Lian just knew that the first one to turn up in a long time would head straight for her. She never went anywhere without a big silk bag containing her secret anti-dragon kit. I don't know what was in it, but even Lian didn't put all her faith in it. Her real plan, when the dreadful day arrived, was to run.

Months passed, and Lian had almost began to stop worrying, when she set off one day for her grandma's house, which was over the hill and through the woods. The hill was very steep, but Lian was fit from all the running practice she did every day. She soon reached the top and set off down the other side. It was then that it happened.

Far below among the trees, there was a great big puff of smoke. And then another one. And then another one. Lian knew at once it wasn't a woodman's fire. It was moving! It was moving more quickly than anything she had ever seen.

There was absolutely no doubt in Lian's mind. There was an enormous dragon down there.

But even as she turned to run, Lian had another thought. Her grandma was down there, too. And she couldn't run very fast at all. Lian was frightened of dragons, but she loved her grandma very much. Without thinking about it too hard, she set off down the hill toward the smoke, clutching her anti-dragon kit.

The smoke had stopped moving now, but the dragon was making a dreadful noise, roaring and panting down in the valley. Lian ran faster. When she reached her grandma's house, she rushed in without knocking.

"Ah, here you are!" said Grandma. "Isn't this exciting?"

Exciting? Being eaten alive? Exciting? But Grandma had grabbed Lian's hand and was dragging her out of the house.

The panting and roaring got louder as Grandma hurried along, and when Lian looked up, she found that the dragon's smokey breath was all around.

"There it is!" cried Grandma. "The very latest way to travel. It's called a train. Hurry! It's about to leave!"

Years later, Lian told her own children about the dragon that was a train. They smiled at her silliness and shook their heads. But then, they didn't know *their* children would one day ride in a dragon that could fly, did they?

Don't Look Behind You!

Fred Rabbit was tired of taking his cousin Nibbles to school. Nibbles was a whining, frightened young rabbit, who imagined foxes behind every bush and owls on every gate post. The trouble was that with such a vivid imagination, he never noticed when there really was something dangerous ahead. Fred had pulled him out of ditches and disentangled him from fences more times than he cared to remember. One evening, on the way home from school, he decided to teach Nibbles a lesson.

Just as the two young rabbits were passing the spooky oak tree at the corner of the lane, Fred paused dramatically and hissed, "Don't look behind you, Nibbles!"

"W-w-why not?" stuttered Nibbles.

"Because I'm pretty sure we're being followed by a Hoojymop," said Fred, "and you don't want to meet a Hoojymop on a Monday."

"W-w-why not?" asked Nibbles, trembling to his toes.

"Because although Hoojymops are cuddly, friendly creatures all the rest of the week," whispered Nibbles, "on Monday nights, they have to eat rabbit pie. It's the Hoojymop law."

Nibbles was so frightened he could hardly walk. "W-w-w-what can we do?" he stammered. "I d-d-don't want to be a p-p-pie!"

"Just keep walking," said Fred, "and keep looking ahead. If we're lucky, we'll see a fox or an owl."

"L-l-l-lucky?" gasped Nibbles. "Why would we want to see one of them?"

"Because they love to eat Hoojymops," explained Fred, "better than they love to eat bunnies. Keep a sharp lookout!"

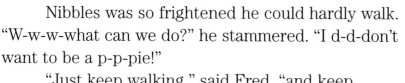

But although both little bunnies peered into the gloom, they didn't see a fox or an owl, and they reached home safely.

It wasn't until they were washing their paws before supper that Nibbles suddenly let out a piercing squeak. "It's Tuesday!" he yelled. "Fred, that Hoojymop wouldn't have eaten us after all."

"Nothing will eat us if you use your head , Nibbles," said Fred, "like you're using it now. If you think about what frightens you, you can make it go away. Even a Hoojymop."

247

Doctor Do-A-Lot

When Doctor Do-A-Lot came calling, it was like a hurricane blowing through the house. He zoomed in through the front door, rushed upstairs to the patient, hummed and haahed, and dashed back down again before you could say, "Good morning, Doctor, fine weather we're having." In fact, before you said "Good…" he thrust a piece of paper into your hand and whirled down the front path, waving his top hat.

The piece of paper was one of Doctor Do-A-Lot's famous prescriptions. Some of them were the kind of thing you would expect.

Measles mixture
2 teaspoonfuls 4 times a day.
Dr. Do-A-Lot

Tonsil tablets
Take two before breakfast.
Dr. Do-A-Lot

Pimple pills
Take two for every pimple that appears.
Dr. Do-A-Lot

Others were a little stranger.

Tummy treatment
Run to the big oak tree and back four times a day until thinner.
Dr. Do-A-Lot

Miseries medicine
Visit Colin the Clown and watch him put his boots on.
Dr. Do-A-Lot

Laziness lotion
Help Mrs Marvel with the washing for her fourteen children.
Dr. Do-A-Lot

Moping measures
Ask Miss Elgar to teach you to play the trombone.
Dr. Do-A-Lot

Everyone in Elftown loved Doctor Do-A-Lot, so you can imagine how upset they were when they heard that the doctor himself was not feeling well. Several elves went to visit him and found him lying in bed, looking pale and ill. But when they asked if he had toothache, or tummy ache, or fidgety feet, he said no. He didn't, he said, have anything that could be found in his medical books. He was as puzzled as anyone else about what was wrong with him.

The elves were worried. They were worried about Doctor Do-A-Lot and they were worried about themselves. What would happen when they needed the doctor? Everywhere you went in Elftown there were elves whispering together on street corners. Because they were whispering, it was some time before Old Mrs Mapleleaf heard about the problem, for her ears were not as sharp as they had once been. But when she was told what had happened, she let out a cackle and began to scribble on a piece of paper.

"Take this to Doctor Do-A-Lot," she said. "He'll soon get better."

And when the doctor saw the paper, he burst into laughter and shooed everyone out of his house.

"I need to get some rest," he said. "I'll see you all next week."

And the paper? Doctor Do-A-Lot framed it and put it on his wall. It said:

Doctor Do-Too-Much's medicine

Take twelve hours of rest every day, mixed with proper meals and a dash of common sense.

Mrs Mapleleaf

Little Cousin Clare

When Bryn heard that his little cousin Clare was coming to visit, he was very excited. He lived on a farm, a long way from the nearest village, and he didn't have any brothers or sisters. Straight away, he began to plan the games he would play with Clare.

Bryn got out all his trucks and cars and arranged them in a line. He decided Clare could choose first which to play with, although he couldn't help hoping it wouldn't be the big blue one. Next he organized all his painting things. He piled stacks of bright paper on the table and lined up his paints and brushes.

"I'm glad to see you're tidying up, Bryn," said Dad, when he came in from the fields. "Your playroom looks much better now."

But Bryn hadn't finished. He started to sort out his books and put all the ones about animals and all the ones about trucks together. He wondered for a moment if Clare would like different kinds of books, as she was a girl, but he couldn't imagine anyone not liking animals and trucks. After all, his mother was always driving the big tractors on the farm.

Last of all, Bryn made a big effort to organize his building bricks. It took ages because he had lots of them. Finally, he was ready.

Bryn was too excited to eat much breakfast the next day. He was waiting for the sound of wheels in the driveway. They came, of course, the moment he wasn't looking out of the window. When he heard his mother flinging open the door and shouting above the noise of the car, Bryn ran up behind her and tried to peep around her legs for his first sight of Clare. All he could see was a lady carrying something wrapped up in a blanket.

"Bryn," smiled his mother, "I want to introduce you to your Aunt Jo."

Aunt Jo bent down. "And I want to introduce you to your little cousin Clare," she said.

Bryn looked right into the face of a tiny, sleeping baby.

"Um… Excuse me," he said. "I just have to put some things away."

"He's been very tidy recently," his mother told Aunt Jo. "He's growing up so fast."

As Bryn put away his trucks, his painting things, his books and his bricks, he didn't really feel bad that Clare couldn't play with them. It meant he had a little more time to have the big blue truck all to himself. He would lend her his big blue bear instead. After all, there's nothing like a baby to make you feel much more grown-up than you've ever been before.

A Christmas Concert

As Christmas drew nearer, the little mice who lived among the roots of the oak tree became more and more excited. Every evening, they twirled together red and orange leaves to make garlands. They drew their own Christmas cards and counted out their tiny mouse money to make sure they had enough to buy presents for friends and families. On the Friday before Christmas, Mrs Mouse was taking them shopping at the edge of the forest. They couldn't wait.

But two weeks before Christmas, it began to snow. The big white flakes floated down thick and fast. The little mice jumped up and down with excitement. It was going to be a white Christmas, and there would be sledging and skating and snowballs!

All week it snowed. On Thursday evening, Mrs Mouse called the little mice to her and spoke seriously.

"I'm sorry, my dears," she said, "but the snow through the forest is so thick, we won't be able to visit the shops tomorrow."

The little mice looked at each other. What about the presents they had planned to buy?

"You are clever little mice," said Mrs Mouse. "I'm sure you could make your own presents if you tried hard."

The little mice worked hard for the next few days, and they were surprisingly good at making presents. They made little acorn bowls and paper planes. They threaded seeds to make necklaces and painted pretty pictures. By Christmas Eve, all the presents were made, except one.

"What are we going to make for Great Aunt Mouse?" they asked.

The trouble with great aunts and grandmothers and other wise old mice is that they already have everything they need. They have more acorn bowls and necklaces and pictures than you can imagine.

"Well, think about what she likes," suggested Mrs Mouse.

"She likes music," said one little mouse.

"She likes little mice," said another.

"We could put on a special Christmas Concert for her!" said a third.

And that is exactly what they did. While the snow drifted down outside, the little mice sang carols, played their drums and whistles, and danced a special Christmas dance. It was a huge success. Every year since, the little mice have entertained all the grown-up mice as far as the edge of the forest and back (if it's not snowing too hard).

I Can't Fall Down!

The monkeys were chattering in the trees and bright sunlight was splashing the glossy leaves of the forest. Mrs Parrot took her youngest son out on a branch and told him what he had to do.

"Just uncurl your feet and let go, Percy," she said. "And then flap your wings as hard as you can."

Percy peered through the leaves. "Mamma," he said, "I can't fall down!"

"It's not a question of falling down, Percy," said his mother sharply. "It's a question of flying. Your sisters can do it. Your brothers can do it. Every single one of your relatives can do it – except your little cousins and they're still in their eggs. Now, don't be a baby. Just let go."

But Percy was not convinced. "Monkeys don't fly," he said. "Snakes don't fly. Even elephants don't fly."

"And thank goodness for that!" cried Mrs Parrot. "No, Percy, none of those animals, poor things, can fly. But parrots can! You can! Go on!"

Percy lifted one foot. Then he lifted the other foot (but he put the other one down first).

"That's just shuffling," said Mrs Parrot. "It's not swooping, or twirling, or flying. Come on, Percy. I've got lots to do this morning."

But Percy simply wouldn't let go. When his mother gave him an encouraging nudge, he clung on tightly with his little feet. He wobbled. He wibbled. But he didn't let go. Mrs Parrot sighed and left him to it.

"You were quite right," said a voice near Percy's ear. It was a young monkey, swinging from a nearby branch. "It's much better being a monkey and not flying," said the new friend. "Just follow me!" And the monkey strolled off along the branch.

Percy followed hot on his heels. It was fine! No flying at all! Even when the monkey speeded up a bit, Percy still hopped along confidently. And when the monkey said, "Now, here you have to jump," Percy simply didn't think about it. He jumped.

Oh! Before he knew what was happening, Percy had given a little flap of his wings and was swooping through the leaves. He tried a twirl. He tried a dive. He tried a double somersault with spin and back flip. It was wonderful! He was flying.

Mrs Parrot watched proudly from a nearby branch. "Thanks, Mavis," she said to a young monkey who was passing.

"Anytime," laughed Mavis.

By the Light of the Moon

araway on the top of the world, there is a place that is always cold where there is only white snow and the icy sea. There are no trees and no flowers at all. There are only seals and fish and bears. Yes, there are big white, furry bears. And when those polar bears are about, the seals and the fish need to watch out, because those bears can creep ever so quietly…

and slide ever so slippily… and run ever so quickly… and dive down into the blue sea with hardly a splash.

"I love that the sun shines all the time and makes the snow sparkly," one little bear told his mother.

"In the winter," said his mother, "the sun doesn't shine at all. Not in the daytime and not in the nighttime."

It wasn't very long before the sun began to go away for part of the day. Then, one night, the little bear woke up and everything around him was blue and velvety.

"What has happened?" he asked his mother.

"The sun has gone away until next year," she replied. "It is winter now. The moon will keep us company all through the winter, until the sun comes again."

The little bear gave a huge sigh. There wasn't anything to worry about. In the daytime and the nighttime, in the summer and the winter, he still lived in a wonderful world.